pieces of me

pieces of me

A Novel

Mary Beth Eversole

"I believe in reincarnation. I believe we're here to learn and grow. We choose how we come into this life based on what it is we have to learn. Some people have harder lessons than others."

—Gillian Anderson

Chapter One

Anya

The woman kneeled beside the ailing child. A dry, desert wind whipped around her as she lay her hands on the child's forehead and abdomen. Another woman stood nearby crying softly: the child's mother.

This child is burning up. If I do not learn what is wrong, I will lose her.

The thought ran through the concerned woman's head as she closed her eyes and desperately called out to the cause of the fever.

As she floated her hands over the little one's listless body, images appeared to her from the long trek the villagers had endured to move from their Siberian home to this new warmer, drier land. The people had been dying. The woman had needed to make a choice: guide her people away from the only home they ever knew or remain and watch her people die. The child stirred in pain and gave a soft whimper. A flash of a man's face came through. He had been one of their strongest warriors, but this view was of his gaunt cheekbones, of the frostbitten lesions that eventually took his life.

Her father. She's mourning the loss of her father, and it is killing her.

"Myosotis. And elderberry." The woman motioned to the mother. "Inchi, we must hurry."

The mother, Inchi, with fear in her eyes, nodded and followed the woman, Anya, the village medicine woman and leader, into her hut.

Chapter Two

Katie

Katie gasped awake. In the darkness of her small bedroom, she slowly came to sense the whir of the fan, the shadowy shapes of the books and journal on her bedside table. She felt the warmth of her fiancé next to her and realized she was soaked in sweat, tangled in the queen-sized sheet they shared.

What was that? she thought as she slowly sat up and cleared the sleep from her eyes.

She vividly remembered the dream. It was so real. Every detail, from the desert wind to the feel of her dry hands on the little girl's burning forehead. But they had not been her hands, really—they had belonged to the forty-year-old tribal woman, Anya. The leader of the village.

What had she been doing? Trying to determine why the girl was so sick. She was a healer.

But it felt so real. It felt to Katie like she *had* been the woman, that those were *her* hands. The power and sense of *knowing* she'd felt in that dream was something she had never experienced before in her waking life.

If only I could feel that way for real. To have that strength. I'd finally know why I'm here. Katie shook her head, clearing the thought from her mind.

"You're here because you're alive and this is your lot in life, Katie."

As she said it out loud, her fiancé stirred and mumbled, "Katie, go to bed, it's still dark."

"Sorry, babe. Go back to sleep."

Katie stared at Chad, wondering how she'd ended up with this man. He was so good to her, but she still felt like something was missing. Something wasn't right. Katie slipped out of bed and into her slipper socks. She quietly padded out of the room and closed the door behind her, the memories of the medicine woman still haunting her.

What happened to her people? Why did that father die and why was his daughter sick now? What is my role in it? HER role?

Katie shook her head again as the confusing thought wracked her brain. Why did she feel so connected to this person who had clearly lived thousands of years ago?

Chester, Katie's white-as-snow cat, rubbed on her legs as she made her way to the kitchen to grab a glass of water. The harsh light of the fridge as she opened it brought her fully awake.

"It was just a dream, Katie," she said out loud.

Chester mewed loudly next to her.

"You're right, Ches. I do need to get a grip." Katie poured herself a cold glass of water and put the filtered pitcher back into the fridge. Plunged back into darkness, she quickly reached for the light switch and flipped it on. She had never been a fan of the dark.

As she made her way to the couch to find the TV remote, she suddenly had an urge to go to her desk where her laptop sat open. Chester bumped her along the way, signaling his desire for breakfast.

"It's too early, Ches. Here, come sit on my lap." She set down her water and patted her thighs as she sat at her desk. Chester made a *hrrrupmh* sound and jumped onto her thighs, purring.

"See? A warm lap is better than a midnight snack, right?" Chester looked up at her ruefully and proceeded to give himself a bath.

"Or at least second best, apparently." She smiled at him and pet his soft head.

Placated by the momentary distraction, Katie opened her laptop, determined to figure out why she had dreamed about a woman from 210 B.C.

How the hell do I know that date? she thought as she typed in "tribal migration 210 B.C." Somehow she knew this was what would give her at least the start of the information she sought.

The screen popped up with multiple searches, but what caught her eye was the map to the right. A red line traced the migration pattern of a tribe that went from the Bering Strait into North America. She clicked on the map.

Once loaded, a large map of Northern America, before it was settled, showed the various migration patterns of old tribes of the region. As she read the caption below it, shivers ran down her spine:

"The Old Bering Sea Culture were small tribes that migrated from Siberia through the Bering Strait into North America to escape the freezing climate killing their people. Some of those tribes still exist today."

I already knew this, Katie thought as she navigated the migration trail with her mouse arrow.

"My people were dying, and I had to get them to warmer climates," she spoke aloud. "The little girl, her father died because of the freezing temperatures. We were trapped and had to get out fast."

She snapped the computer lid shut, confused. She squeezed her eyes shut and shook her head. *How do I know this? It's so real. I* know *it—it wasn't just a dream.*

Chills shook her again as she placed the laptop on the side table and stood. Chester *hrrumph*-ed to the ground, having been disturbed from his nap in her lap.

Katie walked back to the bedroom door, and Chester stared up at her, annoyed that he had been so rudely woken only to find that breakfast was not going to be served after all.

"Sorry, Ches, I think I need some more sleep. I'm thinking things that aren't real."

But they are real, she thought as she softly opened the door and snuck back into bed. Chad rolled over and snuggled into her, and she gratefully snuggled back. She needed to feel that comfort, that realness.

It was just a dream, go back to sleep. This she told herself as she tried to listen to Chad's slow breathing and calm herself back into sleep.

The last thing she remembered before she fell into slumber yet again was the face of the little girl as the woman desperately tried to revive her.

Chapter Three

Katie

"Katie! . . . Katie? . . .Vanilla oat milk latte with extra foam for Katie!"

The barista looked around and finally gave up and set the drink on the counter, going back to her work. Katie snapped to at the final callout for her drink. The glow of her laptop bathed her in blank white light, open to the page that had only a cursor blinking at the top. She's been lost in thought for ten minutes, but she had not been thinking about the column she was supposed to be writing for *The Weekly Word*, a newspaper about local life in Phoenix. The column was supposed to be about café culture, the artists who flock to local restaurants like the one she was currently in, and the creativity that is manifested there, but all she could think about was Anya.

Get a grip, Katie.

She noticed a young girl approaching the counter and about to grab Katie's drink so she stood and walked quickly to the counter.

"Sorry, I think that's my drink, sweetie," Katie said gently.

The girl startled, whipped around to stare at Katie for an instant, and then ran out of the shop. In those few seconds, Katie got a glimpse of a young face—dirty, gaunt, as if the little girl hadn't eaten in days . . . and eerily similar to the little girl she had seen in her dream.

"Wait!" Katie shouted as the little one bolted out of the store.

Katie left her drink and followed the girl outside. Her face—it had been just like the little girl's face her hands had been cupping in the dream. Katie had to find her.

Her heart rate quickened as she caught a glimpse of the girl's long, straggly black hair and faded pink T-shirt.

"Hey! Sweetie!" Katie tried to run after her, but the girl disappeared into the crowd of the crossing pedestrian traffic. Katie reached the other side of the street and circled, desperately looking for the pink T-shirt, the imploring eyes she had just witnessed.

She's gone. I've lost her. A remarkable sense of failure and sadness, something familiar to Katie in recent months, washed over her as she trudged back to the café. *I've lost her again.*

Tears welled in her eyes as she sat down at her computer, which thankfully was still there. The barista walked up and placed a drink in front of Katie.

"I saw what happened. That girl is always lurking around here. She's gotten away with a few people's drinks before. Sorry about that. I remade this for you."

Katie stared up at the barista in a fog and accepted the drink.

"Thank you."

The barista began to walk away.

"Wait!" Katie yelped.

The barista turned, a slight look of annoyance on her face.

"Do you know her name? Are her parents with her?"

"No, I'm pretty sure she's homeless. Constantly begging people for things outside our door. Sometimes she manages to sneak in and grab something when we're busy. We've tried to help her before, but she always runs when we approach her. Some people just don't want help."

"She's just a child," Katie said emphatically.

"What do you want me to do? Chase her down and make her tell me who she is and where she comes from? Lady, we're busy here. We do what we can. Enjoy the drink." The barista huffed away quickly and left Katie to her brooding.

She's just a child, she thought as she took a sip of her drink, burning her tongue in the process.

Her phone rang. She looked at the name and sighed.

"Oh man." She pressed accept. "Hello, this is Katie."

"Katie, what the hell?!" Her boss, Sam, yelled into the phone. "Where's your article? It was due this morning! We're having to scramble to fill the space because I haven't been able to reach you since Monday!"

Katie pulled her phone away from her face to look at her recent calls. Ten missed calls from Sam since yesterday. *Crap.*

"Sam, I'm so sorry. I've been . . . Something came up that needed my attention, and I had to put it on hold. I'm finishing it up right now." Katie stared at the blank page on her screen as she told the lie. "It'll be to you by the end of the hour." She silently cursed as she gave herself a deadline she knew she wouldn't be able to meet with anything remotely acceptable.

"It better be! This is the third time this has happened, Katie. What's going on with you? You used to be one of our best writers and now you turn in half-assed assignments, late almost every time. I can't keep vouching for you if this is how it's gonna be from now on. The guys upstairs are ready to put my head on a platter! So whatever it is that's distracting you, figure it out and get your head back in the game, or we're gonna be having a different conversation. You got it?"

"Yeah." The threat, wrapped in the clichés so typical of her boss, sat like a stone on her heart. The guilt she had felt outside deepened into shame. This is not who she was. "I'm sorry, Sam. I'll do better. You'll have the article."

"Good. Get going. And Katie, you know I'm here if you need to talk. If not me, then talk to someone, okay? I hate to see a good writer go down in flames because of poor decisions. Get some help, okay?"

"Sure, okay." The anger Katie felt inside pierced her heart, like a dagger. She stuffed it down, deep, and inhaled. "I'm working on it. I need to get back to my article."

"By the end of the hour. I mean it, Katie."

"Got it." Katie numbly hung up the phone.

Get yourself together, Katie, you cannot afford to lose this job.

But what's the point?

The small voice inside was faint, but it was there, asking the same question she'd been asking for months now. What she used to love didn't bring her the same joy anymore. She knew this was a dream job that most writers would give anything for, but she just couldn't bring herself to feel anything about it anymore. What was the point of writing about creative café culture when starving, unhoused children were being chased out of those same cafés with threats instead of invited in for a meal? What was the point when you try so hard to have a baby of your own only to have it die in your womb?

"Stop it. Stop thinking about it," Katie whispered to herself as she discovered she was gripping her abdomen. She sighed. She turned toward her keyboard and typed:

"Creative Café Culture and Its Impact on Life as We Know It."

She began to write. But it wasn't the assignment she originally planned; it became something more. As she wrote, she found herself asking those very questions she had been pondering. She wove the story of her experience with the girl in the café earlier that hour among the other stories and observations she had gathered over the past week about the deluge of creatives flocking to small cafés like this to find the creative flow. Between the stories of artists being discovered and their art being featured on the walls of the café, Katie peppered the bigger questions: What were we all here for? If the point is to create with fellow human beings, to reach a higher level of understanding, how could we let this little girl slip through the cracks? Shouldn't she be the reason we are doing it all in the first place? Shouldn't she be the focus of our art? Human suffering is a fact, so shouldn't the end of human suffering be the creative's cause? And if it really starts at a table in a small café in Phoenix, shouldn't the little girl who frequents said café just to find her next meal or drink be the catalyst instead of the bane of the customers sitting beside her trying to ignore her?

Katie finished her article, and before she could stop herself, she pressed send.

If I'm going to lose my job, I'm going to lose it writing about what I think should be said.

She closed her laptop, finished the last sip of her latte, stood, and exited the café, a weight having been lifted off her shoulders. Today was the first day she felt she had really written well in a long time.

If a single dream can do this for me, then I wonder what else I can learn from my dreams?

She decided to find out.

Chapter Four

Jenice

The little girl could feel her heart racing as she bolted from the shop. The lady had seen her. She knew she'd be in trouble if she was caught, so she ran, just like always. But something about that lady was different. She didn't seem mad; she seemed like she wanted to ask her something. Jenice didn't stick around to find out. She knew what came from sticking around: a call to social services, a car ride, strangers (sometimes nice, sometimes not), or worse, the bars of the detention centers.

As she was running across the street, she bumped into a person and spun around. The lady was still coming after her, yelling! She ran faster, bent down so she fit into the crowd more, and at the first sign of a corner, she turned. It brought her to an entryway of a closed store. She hid behind the stone wall and peered out to see if the lady was still following her. She wasn't. She was turning in a circle on the corner, looking for her, but not seeing her.

That was close. I'll have to be faster next time, Jenice thought as she watched the woman drop her arms in defeat and walk back toward the café.

Jenice's stomach gave a painful rumble, reminding her that she had not accomplished what she went into the café for in the first place. She hadn't eaten in a couple days and had already finished the water bottle a nice man had given her on the street yesterday when she was begging. She felt a little faint and sat on the pavement.

Food.

She looked around for any trashcans and noticed a large dumpster down the alley across the street from her. Today would be a dumpster-diving day. She hated those days. Her stomach rumbled again, reminding her she had to do it. She forced herself upright and started across the street.

I miss Mommy.

A flash of hands pulling her away from her mother went through her head. Cries of anguish and angry yelling. Dogs barking. Tears threatened to burst from her eyes. Jenice shook her head in resolve and continued toward the dumpster. Mommy said she would come for me. I just have to be strong. She climbed up on a crate next to the dumpster, opened the lid, crawled up to the edge, and jumped in.

Chapter Five

Sarah

Sarah opened her eyes. Pain seared through her head as she tried to register where she was. It was dark. Cold rain pelted her face. Light splayed horizontally from somewhere over her broken body as a man held her head in his lap.

"Hey, hey, stay awake. What's your name?" he said as he grabbed her hand. She could tell from the look on his face that something was terribly wrong.

Sarah felt the hand, heard his voice through what sounded like a distant ringing. She tried to speak, but pain shot through her neck as the attempt failed. She coughed.

She felt something trickle down the side of her mouth. *Blood?* There was sharp pain all across her forehead, like she was being stabbed with several needles at once.

"Jesus." She heard the man swear under his breath. His face looked forlorn as he squared his shoulders and gave a slight shake of his head. She felt him gently wipe her chin, she could see there was, indeed, blood as he pulled his hand away from her face. Sarah gave a whimper as she began to feel pain in her leg. She couldn't tell for sure, but it felt like it was bent at the wrong angle. She tried to glance down to see and was met with the view of a jagged piece of the car's windshield sticking out from her torso. She cried out in fear.

"It's okay. It's going to be okay. Can you tell me your name?" the man said kindly.

Sarah made an effort again, and a sound like a wisp of air came out with the word "Sarah."

"Sarah. It's okay, you don't have to keep talking. I'm Jim." She could see that he was holding back tears, and that he swallowed hard. "Sarah, you've been in an accident with me. I think you may have been trying to avoid something in the road or maybe you fell asleep for a second. You veered over to my lane. I'm so sorry, I didn't have time to react. We hit each other. You came through the windshield."

Sarah saw Jim wince for a moment and noticed that he had an injured arm and a gash on his face.

"I tried calling for help on my CB radio, but so far no one is answering. I'll try again in a minute."

Sarah coughed again and tasted the coppery tang of blood. As she watched Jim look up into the rain for a minute, she heard him whisper, "God help me."

She felt a pang of terror run through her. He looked back down at her.

"Don't you worry about a thing, Sarah. I'm here with you, okay? It's going to be okay. Just hold on to me. If you feel tired, that's okay, you can close your eyes. I'll be here with you. I'm not going to leave you."

Sarah registered the words he was saying.

I'm dying. That's what he's telling me. I'm dying. This is it. Why didn't I go into the diner? Why didn't I just go in and talk to her?

"MMM-Ahhh," Sarah cried out. She was crying for her mother. She felt Jim squeeze her hand.

"Shhhh. It's okay, Sarah. I'm here. You'll be okay."

Sarah closed her eyes for an instant, a tear running down her cheek.

"Sarah? Are you still with me? I'm still here. You're not alone."

She could still feel him holding her hand, but when she opened her eyes and tried to nod, she found she could not feel her face anymore. She realized the lights streaming onto her were from his truck's headlights. She had hit a large truck. She was dying. Suddenly the light became brighter. It filled the sky. She could no longer feel anything. Everything became warm.

She knew instinctively that the rain was cold and that the kind man was still next to her, but she felt only the warmth. She saw him mouth the words as light enveloped him, too:

"It's okay, Sarah. You can go. It's okay."

Then, she could no longer hear or see him. All she saw was the light. She became the light.

Chapter Six

Katie

Katie shot up in her bed. The familiar dream haunted her as she shook sleep from her head. It was the most she had ever seen and heard in the dream. Normally it ended with her dying, but this time she wasn't just experiencing it as the woman; she'd floated out of the body and became an observer after her death. Katie had watched silently as Sarah's body shuddered one last breath. She saw her grip Jim's hand tightly. He gripped back. Then just like that, she was still, her eyes went dull, her head turned to the side. Sarah was gone.

"Oh God. Oh God! Sarah? Sarah?!" Katie heard Jim exclaim as she saw tears flow freely down his face while he gently removed himself from holding Sarah's lifeless body. He set her head on the pavement and stood. Katie saw him turn to his truck and realize he was covered in Sarah's blood as he whispered, "Dear God."

She saw him walk to the cab, reach for his CB radio, and make another call.

"Is anyone out there? Anyone? This is Breaker- 42. There's been an accident."

Katie could hear a distant static-filled voice respond, "Breaker-42 this is Breaker-70. What is your twenty? I'll alert the authorities."

She watched, heartbroken, as Jim looked one more time at the body of Sarah lying in a pool of blood, glass, and metal on the pavement then turned and put his head in his hand.

"We're close to the juncture of A-road 4 and B-road 28. Please send help. She's gone. The woman, Sarah, she's gone."

She'd been having this dream since she could remember, around the age of five. Always the same: she was lying on the pavement of a dark road in the rain. She was in a powder blue dress and had red hair. Somehow, she knew she was a singer and was on her way to a gig. Something had caused her to swerve into oncoming traffic, and while this road was normally deserted at that time of night, on this particular night, a large truck had been headed her way. They collided. She'd been thrown from the car. She had woken up with her head supported by a stranger who had stayed with her until she died. And that is where the dream always ended. Until now.

What is happening to me?

Somehow this time, she knew she had been distracted. She had just come from seeing her mother through a diner window. The mother who had abandoned her and her siblings years before. She had not seen her since, but there she was. And she wanted to go to her, to talk to her, ask her why, tell her she finally understood a little because of what she, Sarah, had just been through, but instead she had kept walking to her car and didn't look back. And then she had died.

Something about the dream scared Katie.

Why did I understand and accept my mom abandoning me? What had I done myself to be able to understand her decision?

Katie shook her head again. Chad stirred next to her.

"Sweetie, are you okay?" he asked.

"Huh? Oh yeah, just can't sleep."

He sat up and tried to gather her in his arms. "Seems to be happening a lot lately. Is it because of the baby? Maybe we should talk about it."

She pushed out of his arms and stood, knocking her knee into her bedside table. The mountain of books toppled, and Katie swore under her breath as she rubbed her knee. She leaned over to pick up the books.

Chad reached over and rubbed her back. "Are you okay, Katie?"

As she placed the sci-fi novel she was currently reading onto the precarious pile atop the brown bedside table her father had built, she once again stepped away from Chad. She was unable to look him in the eye.

"I'm fine."

Sadness crossed Chad's face as his hand fell limply onto the blue bedspread they had shared for five years now.

"I'm just worried about you, Katie. We need to talk about it." Chad hesitated at the next statement, trying to catch Katie's eye. "Or if you won't talk to me, I think you need to talk to someone."

At this, Katie whipped around and glared at him. The sun was just beginning to shine through the window behind him, a steady gleam setting over his head like a halo. He really was one of kindest people she knew, but in this moment, the anger was so strong that she didn't care.

"What is it with all the men in my life thinking I need to go talk to someone?!" Katie snapped. She worked her way around the edge of the bed toward the door.

Chad looked shocked and a bit hurt. "Just because you think you can just pick up and move on doesn't mean you can. Doesn't mean we can. We have to deal with this." He reached for her again.

"I'm fine. I just need some space, okay? Go back to sleep." Katie shied away from his touch and opened the door. Chad sighed.

"At some point, Katie, we're going to have to face this together. Or else—"

"Or else what? Jesus, Chad! You're not the one who had to birth a stillborn child out of your body! I need some goddamn space, okay?"

Shocked at her own words, Katie felt the weight of what she had said hang in the air between them. Outside, a shadow covered the sun. It was as though all the light in the world was diminished. She tried desperately to hide the pain she was feeling and hoped that it wasn't showing on her face. The last thing she wanted to do was make Chad feel bad for something that wasn't his fault.

Chad laid back down, chastised. "Okay. Fine." He rolled over and pulled the covers atop him.

Fighting back tears, Katie turned and left the bedroom, shutting the door behind her. Chester greeted her by looping through her legs, rubbing up against her and purring. Through her tears, Katie picked him up and hugged him tight. His warmth and buzzing motor eased her anxiety a bit.

"At least you don't tell me what I need." Katie held him tight. He squirmed and jumped out of her arms, throwing an annoyed look back at her. She laughed. "Only what *you* need, I guess."

She sat down in front of her laptop and opened it to find the article she had written about the little girl. A flash of the girl from the Anya dream entered her mind, then a flash of the face of Sarah's mother, and another little girl, bedraggled, surrounded by siblings in the shack they lived in, watching this same mother leave them through the front door, never to return. Katie closed her eyes for a moment.

What is happening to me? Maybe I do need help.

Katie shut the computer. She headed to the brown faux leather couch, sat down, pulled her favorite multicolored fuzzy blanket up to her waist, and turned on the TV. Chester jumped up into her lap and began to purr again. The only things on were infomercials and old sitcoms from the seventies. She chose an old sitcom. As the laugh track played for the cheesy jokes, Katie let her brain shut off for those few moments.

Chapter Seven

Anya

It had been four days since the child had come into Anya's rectangular hut. The cool temperatures of the waning autumn had not infiltrated the hut due to the entrance tunnel being lower than the floor of the hut, trapping the cold air and allowing the child to heal in the relative warmth of the fire built in the center of the hut. Her fever had finally broken that morning, and she was sweating on the pad she was resting on. Still asleep, the little one finally looked at peace. Anya stood and walked over to the fire in the center of the room where a concoction of plants and berries, gathered from the nearby marsh, simmered. Dried herbs and berries hung from vines draped down the sides of her hut. She slowly walked from bunch to bunch, smelling and touching as she went. She was looking for the right plant to wake the child. She didn't want to startle her, but it was time for her to open her eyes and breathe in the fresh air. Anya stopped at the sweet and minty-smelling herb she had gathered only a few days earlier.

Lemon Balm, this is the one.

She pulled it from the wall, walked to the pile of clay pots the village women had made for her after the migration, and dropped the dried leaves into one. With a pestle fashioned from a chiseled slate rock, she crushed the leaves until they were in fine pieces. Then she grabbed the pot of heated water hanging from a wooden scaffolding over the fire and poured it into the dried mixture to form a thick paste. Dipping her fingers into the bowl, she brought them out covered in the paste and spread them over the upper lip of the child.

"Yaari," Anya gently coaxed the child by nudging her shoulder. "Yaari, it is time to wake up."

Yaari's eyelids fluttered and then opened. She gazed at the ceiling and then began to look around the hut, confused.

"Yaari, you are in the healing hut. You've been very ill."

"Momma?" the child cried out, desperate for her mother.

"Inchi is nearby. She has gone to gather more berries so you would have something to eat when you woke. She will return soon."

The child calmed a bit.

"Come, try to sit up." Anya reached her arm around the back of Yaari and helped her sit. The child swayed a bit, disoriented for a moment, but then settled. She looked directly into Anya's eyes.

"My father is dead."

"Yes." Anya felt a pang of guilt as the child stared imploringly at her. "Yes, he died when we were moving. I am sorry, child. But his spirit is ever with us."

"How?" Yaari, seemingly skeptical but hopeful, asked.

"You know we believe our spirits join the Great Council when they leave this earth. And the Council is ever-present, always watching over us."

"He is there now?"

"Yes, Yaari, he is here." Anya waved her free arm in a wide arc, motioning to the sky. "The Great Council is in all the world around us. In the plants, in the water, in the sky. There are spirits everywhere. The good spirits, like your father, protect us from the bad. Your father is a warrior, even in death and beyond."

The child seemed to take some comfort in that and began to truly look around the hut, curious. Dried plants hung everywhere. There was a fire in the center of the hut, where a cauldron sat, stewing. A table to the right of her had various fresh plants and flowers strewn among the bowls and pestles.

"What are all these plants for?"

"You've never been in here, have you?"

Yaari shook her head.

"These are the plants, berries, grasses, and trees that heal those who are sick or ailing."

"Was I sick?"

"Yes. I believe you were dying from a broken heart and a depth of sadness we could not reach for many months. But you are better now. Do you feel the sadness anymore?"

Yaari pondered for a moment. "Not like before. When I think about Papa, it makes me miss him, but I do not feel so bad anymore."

"Good. That is very good." Anya breathed an internal sigh of relief. A sense of self came back to her. *At least I saved the child.*

Anya was a healer, the medicine woman and leader of the village. Losing Yaari's father had been a terrible blow to her confidence and made her second-guess whether she was fit to lead the village anymore. But saving this child had restored her faith in her abilities. She knew she could watch over her people, just as Yaari's father's spirit now watched over all of them.

"Can I stir this?" Yaari's excited tone brought Anya out of her thoughts. The child was standing next to the cauldron now.

"Yes. Would you like to know what it is?"

The child nodded as she happily grabbed the stone stirring rod, hardly showing any signs of her recent brush with death.

"It is myosotis and elderberry, the concoction that saved your life."

The child's eyes went wide as she looked in the pot.

"These flowers and berries can do that?"

Anya laughed. "Yes, Mother Earth is the true healer, isn't she?"

Yaari nodded again. "Can I learn how to do this?"

Anya stopped and thought for a moment. Could she? Could this child be her apprentice? Anya was getting older and knew she would not last forever. And what then for her people? Who would take over as healer and leader? This precocious child, who fought her way back from the brink of death, could be the answer. As she prepared to answer, Inchi, Yaari's mother, came into the hut, arms full of flowers and berries.

"Momma!"

Inchi dropped her bundle and fell to her knees with tears of relief as her child ran into her arms.

"Yaari? Oh, Yaari! You're awake!"

As the two embraced, Anya stood watching them, contemplating the child's future.

Yes, now is the time to take on an apprentice.

Chapter Eight

Katie

Katie sat at her familiar spot at the café. It was the best spot in the place because no matter what time of day it was, the sun never hit directly on the table or chairs. She could sit there all day writing, like she had many a time, and never have to move because of light in her eyes. Today was not about writing, though. Today was about confiding in someone she trusted. Aliya Jones, Katie's best friend, sat across from her listening intently.

"I can't shake the feeling that these dreams are real. That somehow I've experienced the things they are going through personally. But that's crazy, right?"

Katie could feel her cheeks flush from embarrassment. Telling someone, even your closest friend, that you're having dreams about living someone else's life and then waking up somehow knowing it was *your* life, is not exactly easy.

"I wouldn't say it's crazy. Unusual, yes, but I've read about things like this."

Aliya Jones was a confident, supremely intelligent professor of psychology and the history of psychology at a prestigious university in town. She was tall, raven-haired, and beautiful inside and out. Always willing to help and loved a good problem to solve. It's part of why Katie loved and admired her so much. She never backed down until the problem was solved. If anyone knew what was going on with these dreams, it would be Aliya.

"Things like what exactly?"

"Like reincarnation dreams—"

"Whoa, you think I'm reliving *actual* past lives in a dream?!"

"Well, possibly."

Katie was dumbfounded for a moment. She'd never really believed the whole "past lives, karma, you come back until you've learned your lesson, cycle of life" thing. However, for some reason, it made sense. She knew she'd been more than just an observer in those dreams. She *felt* what they felt. Thought what they thought. Knew what was going to happen next, as if they were memories replaying in her mind.

"Go on."

"I don't know a lot about it, but essentially, when the universe is trying to urge you in a certain direction, make you see something, learn something, it will start bringing up past life memories to help you along the way." Aliyah took a sip of the bottled water she had purchased from the counter. Katie was mid sip with and almost choked on her vanilla oat milk latte when Aliyah said this.

"So the Universe is telling me I need to die in a car crash?"

Aliyah looked thoughtful as she screwed the cap back onto her bottle and placed it on the table next to the cushy chair she was sitting in.

"Not necessarily. It's the car crash and death that are showing you, possibly warning you, about something in your current life that you need to address or change."

Katie sat quiet for a moment.

"Is there something about the death dream that causes you to think you may need to address something happening now?" Aliya studied Katie's face, then quietly, "I know you've been dealing with a lot since the baby . . ."

"Just before I died, I thought, 'Why didn't I go in and talk to her?'" Katie set her drink down on the round coffee table between them. Suddenly her own cushy chair didn't feel so cushy.

"Talk to whom?" Aliyah looked confused.

Katie squirmed a bit. She felt so nervous to tell her best friend. She realized she was stroking her thigh with her thumb, a comforting movement she did when she was anxious and trying to calm down. Her leg was bouncing, a sign that she was too anxious to control her subconscious movements. Katie could see Aliyah taking note of all these signs when Aliyah pointedly looked at Katie's leg and hand and then back at her, tilting her head slightly, and waiting patiently. Katie felt she couldn't hold it in anymore.

Then it all just came pouring out.

"My mother. The reason I wasn't paying attention and swerved into the truck was because I was thinking about my mother who abandoned me. She had been in a diner across the street from me just before I got in the car to go to my gig. I saw her through the window. I wanted to go in, to ask her why she left, but a part of me understood why and didn't want to hear the answer because I knew it would make me more like her. Like I knew, because of what happened in my own life that made me understand her more, but I don't know what that thing is yet. So I didn't go into the diner. I got in my car and then I got into the accident."

Aliyah raised an eyebrow. "That's a lot for not remembering the dream well."

"That's the thing. This wasn't a dream, Ali. I really did die. I think you're right. I think I'm reliving past lives in my dreams. I don't know why, though."

Aliyah reached over and covered Katie's hand with her own. "You've been through so much recently. I think this may be part of your grieving process. A way to learn more about yourself, to maybe find purpose again."

Tears sprang into Katie's eyes. "How'd you know?"

"I know my best friend. You haven't been yourself since you lost Joshua. You're late on work assignments, you cancel plans the majority of the time. You're agitated, sad, or annoyed every time I see you or talk to you. And it's completely understandable, but you also are not allowing the grief process to happen. You're stuck, sweetie, and that's okay, but you have to start moving through it."

"How? How do I move through the death of my son and repeating dreams about myself dying or trying to save people in the past?"

Aliyah pondered for a moment. She pulled out a bright pink sticky pad and ballpoint pen from her beautifully crafted Coach purse.

"Oh god, the sticky pad." Katie laughed slightly.

"See that's the BFF I know and love." Aliyah wrote out a name and number and handed it to Katie.

"This is a good friend and colleague of mine. She started out in psychology as a private therapist and was on her way to completing her MD to become a psychiatrist when she had a personal tragedy. It changed her completely. She closed her practice and started attending workshops and certification courses for alternative medicine. Now, she's a certified acupuncturist and hypnotherapist. She specializes in past life regression hypnotherapy."

Aliyah grabbed her water bottle, unscrewed the cap, and took another swig. Katie watched her skeptically.

"That's a thing?"

Aliyah smiled.

"I know. It sounds crazy, too. You know I have always been skeptical of the alternative medicine world, but the results she has seen from her patients cannot be denied. I've never taken a past life regression session from her myself, but she is highly regarded in the alternative medicine community. She's written several books on the subject matter of past lives and how they affect your current life. She only takes clients by referral now because she is so busy with touring conferences, but I know she would see you if I put in a referral on your behalf. In fact, I think she would find your case quite interesting."

Katie sighed and smiled slightly at Aliyah.

"You have always taken care of me."

"Hey, it goes both ways. Don't think I will forget this favor."

They laughed. For as long as they could remember, they had always jokingly held each other to the "Favor List." Of course, in reality, they had both helped each other so much there was no way and no point in keeping track, but it was still a running inside joke they shared.

"Oh, I'm pretty sure you still owe me from the last one!" Katie laughed. "Remember that guy from Cabo?"

"Oh god, you're right. Please don't remind me." They laughed out loud.

"He was so convinced you were that famous actress that he followed you to the bathroom to get an autograph!"

"And then you had to step in like you were my security detail so he couldn't get through the . . ."

Katie startled and stood abruptly, almost tripping over the table in front of her while trying to get a better view of the café counter.

"Oh my God, there she is."

"Who? The actual actress?"

Aliyah excitedly turned to see who Katie was looking at. All she saw were two people in line: the barista and a young girl.

"No, the girl I told you about who tried to steal my coffee. There she is!"

Chapter Nine

Katie

For weeks, Katie had waited for the little girl in the café to return, but she had not. Katie was worried she had scared her away from coming back, but then, all of a sudden, there she was. She couldn't cover her excitement.

"There she is! I've got to go try and talk to her." Katie took a step in the direction of the counter.

Aliyah interjected, grabbing Katie's arm. "Whoa, sweetie, do you think that's a good idea? You already chased her down the block. She looks like she hasn't eaten in days and just wants a handout. Why don't you let the barista do that? I've worked with unhoused kiddos before. They are a skittish lot and don't trust people. If you already ran her off once, chances are, when she sees you, she's going to take off running again."

Katie sank back into her overstuffed chair, defeated.

"I just want to see if she's okay. Ask where her parents are. Maybe buy her some lunch. I just don't think it's fair that she's there at what, nine years old, trying to just beg for a piece of food, while I'm here with my vanilla oat milk latte every day like it's nothing."

Katie could feel Aliyah studying her face, considering what she just said.

"You're really serious about this, aren't you?"

"I just don't want to make the same mistake twice. I left without talking to my mom in that dream. I don't want to leave this girl without talking to her."

Katie could feel Aliyah's intense gaze upon her, she could tell her friend was conflicted about how to respond, but Katie knew if she didn't seize this moment, she'd lose the girl forever. She began to stand when suddenly Aliyah put her hand on Katie's arm, halting her.

"Stay right here." Aliyah jumped up and hurried over to the granite counter where the little girl was staring at the delectable food samples through the rounded glass displays.

"Aliyah!" Katie tried to call her back, but she was gone before she could stop her.

Chapter Ten

Jenice

Jenice stared through the glass at the savory and sweet food on display. But it wasn't the food in the case she was after. She looked around to see if anyone was watching. She had spotted an egg sandwich on the counter that no one had picked up that had been sitting for about three minutes. She was timing it to make sure she could grab it and dash before anyone even noticed. Mouth watering, she reached for the sandwich.

"Now that looks tasty, doesn't it? Would you like me to get you one? We should probably leave that one for the customer who bought it, but I was about to order and would love to get you one of your own."

Jenice startled then just stared at the beautiful woman smiling and looking back at her.

She hadn't threatened or yelled. She'd simply spoken to her like she was a normal, everyday customer, or maybe even a friend. That was new.

"Would you like an egg sandwich? I'm an egg and ham fan myself, but whatever floats your boat."

"Floats my boat?" Jenice responded, confused.

"Oh, it's a saying." Laughing, the woman continued, "It means whatever you like is okay."

The child continued to stare at the older woman, not sure if she should answer. But her stomach reminded her how hungry she was.

"I like hamandeggandcheese."

"Well then, ham and egg and cheese it is!" She turned to the cashier and ordered. "One ham and egg sandwich, and one ham, egg, and cheese sandwich please."

The barista looked at the child, clearly recognizing her, a look of pity on her face.

"We are having a feast today. Aren't we . . . um, I didn't get your name. I'm Aliyah."

The beautiful woman had turned to Jenice again while she said this. Normally Jenice didn't tell anyone her name, but this woman was so nice and friendly, she found herself saying, "I'm Jenice. Jenice Abuela."

"Well, Jenice Abuela, it's really nice to meet you. Would you like a drink with your sandwich? I hear the oat lattes are really good!"

Jenice nodded her head and said quietly, "Can I have chocolate milk?"

Aliyah, smiled and said softly, "Of course you can have chocolate milk." She turned back to the cashier and ordered the milk.

"The milk is on the house," the cashier said.

Aliyah smiled and said, "That is really kind of you. Thank you."

"Well, one kindness deserves another right?" The cashier looked to Jenice and winked.

Jenice flinched a little, but then realized the cashier was smiling at her.

"Yes," she quietly responded.

Why were these people being nice to her all of a sudden? Jenice couldn't remember the last time someone had paid her a kindness without wanting something in return. The last time she thought someone was just trying to be nice, maybe, was that woman she ran from in this café a few weeks ago. Since then, Jenice had been avoiding the café because she'd seen the lady there every day and she was embarrassed for having tried to take her drink and then having run from her. She'd known the lady would have given her the drink. She didn't know why she had run in the first place. The lady had just seemed so familiar. Like how her momma made her feel. But her momma wasn't there, and the lady wasn't her momma. The feeling had scared her, like she would be forgetting her real momma if she let another lady take care of her for a moment.

Jenice felt a gentle hand on her shoulder and suddenly the sandwich she ordered was in front of her.

"Here you are, sweet Jenice. Now, you are welcome to take this food and go, but my friend and I would love for you to come sit and have lunch with us if you would like to. Her name is Katie, and I think you two may have met once before."

Jenice looked to where Aliyah was pointing and jumped. There she was, sitting in a light gray cushioned chair across the café: the kind lady she'd been avoiding for weeks. Jenice looked to Aliyah, panicked.

"There are no strings attached, Jenice. You do not have to sit with us or even stay in the café. You can take your food and go. I just wanted to let you know that my friend, Katie, was really worried about you last time you met, and she hasn't stopped thinking about you since. She just wanted to make sure you are okay. She is really nice, and when the lunch is done, you are welcome to go and never see us again if you don't want to. The choice is yours. You can leave or you can stay. I'll let you think about it. I'm going to go sit down with Katie and enjoy this egg and ham sandwich!"

Aliyah left Jenice and went back to sit next to Katie. Jenice just stared for a moment. The woman, Katie, looked so nice, but also kind of sad. She was blonde and was wearing a blue shirt with jeans. Something her momma would wear. Something about the woman made Jenice think maybe it was okay to eat lunch with them. She hadn't eaten lunch with anyone since she'd escaped the center where her momma was.

She decided to sit with them.

Jenice made her way slowly over to their little corner of the café and sat in the chair they had pulled up for her. She noticed Aliyah had shared her sandwich with the nice lady. Momma would have done the same thing. She missed her so much. Katie and Aliyah both smiled at Jenice, and they all dug into their sandwiches in a peaceful silence.

After a few moments, Jenice set her sandwich down.

"Is the sandwich okay?" Katie asked, looking concerned.

Jenice nodded her head, wanting to speak what was on her mind but feeling nervous.

"Is anything bothering you, sweetie? I don't know how much my friend, Aliyah, told you," Katie motioned to Aliyah with a grateful smile, "but my name is Katie. We've met once before, but I'm afraid I may have overreacted a bit that time."

Jenice kept looking at her but nodded her head. "I'm sorry."

Katie looked shocked. "Jenice, you have nothing to be sorry for! I'm the goof who scared the living daylights out of you by chasing you down the street! I didn't mean to. I just wanted to see if you were okay. I would have given you the drink or bought you your own."

"I know." Jenice looked into Katie's eyes, tears welling up.

Gently, Katie continued, "So why are you sorry then? You were just trying to survive."

"I'm sorry because I know you would've given me that drink, and all I had to do was ask. But I ran. And my momma told me never to throw away a kindness. I'm sorry. You kinda remind me of her and I miss her so much and I didn't know what to do so I ran." Tears were spilling over and down Jenice's face now.

Katie and Aliyah exchanged concerned looks. Aliyah put her hand over Jenice's, and Katie came around to her other side and grabbed her up in a gentle hug.

"Sweetheart, you do not need to apologize for anything, especially not for missing your mom. Is she somewhere you can visit her?"

Jenice shook her head. Jenice pulled away from Katie's embrace slightly, so Katie let her go but stayed by her side.

"Jenice, is your momma in danger?" Aliyah watched Jenice's reaction as she asked the question.

Tears began to fall faster. Jenice looked to Katie, who nodded, and then to Aliyah. These ladies were so nice, and she'd been on her own now for what seemed like forever. Maybe they could help.

"I don't know! We came here. Then some bad men took us to a concrete building with fences. They had dogs and they grabbed my momma really hard. I tried to fight them, but one of them picked me up and put me over his shoulder. He carried me away from Momma while the others were taking her inside the building. We were screaming and crying. Momma kept saying 'Stop! Please stop! We are seeking asylum! She is my daughter!' but they wouldn't listen. Before she was gone, Momma looked at me and screamed, 'Corre, bebe, corre, ahora!'" One of the men shoved her hard, shouting to 'shut up with all that Spanish bullshit.'"

Aliyah and Katie both just listened, horrified looks on their faces.

Jenice continued: "The bad man put me down in a little room. I could hear other kids down the hall. I saw a door at the other end of the hall. It was close enough and the man was on the phone. So I did what my momma told me. 'Corre.' I ran."

Katie quietly gasped. "Oh, sweetheart."

"I don't think the man noticed for a while, because I made it outside without anyone seeing. There was a gate at the end of the fence that trucks were coming in and out of. I hid behind a large trash bin and waited until the gate opened and a truck was leaving. Then I ran next to the truck, and I was out. I didn't know where to go. There were some trees close by, so I ran there and hid for a little while. I was so scared they would find me. All I wanted to do was go find Momma, but she had told me to run. So I kept running."

"How did you end up here, Jenice?" Aliyah asked.

"A woman saw me at the train station. My momma had said we needed to go to Pheonix. That we would be safe there. She asked where my momma and papi were. I thought she might take me back to the bad men, so I lied and told her I had visited my abuela and was taking the train back to Momma and Papi in Pheonix, but I had lost my ticket and didn't have any money. She asked if I knew their phone number so she could call them, but I said I couldn't remember, only that I was supposed to meet them at the Phoenix train station. She bought me another ticket and rode with me to Phoenix. She had to keep going on the train, so when I got off the train, I ran up to a man and a woman and hugged them to make it look like they were my momma and papi. They were so surprised that they just hugged back for a few seconds. The train started to leave, and I could see the lady watching me, so I ran with the train to wave to her. Then I just kept running and left the station."

"That was very quick thinking on your part, Jenice. You really know how to survive."

Jenice could see the concern on Aliyah's face.

"Did anyone help you after that, Jenice? Maybe the couple you hugged?"

Jenice noticed that Katie looked very concerned at this point.

"No, I ran from them as soon as the train started moving. I went outside. There were so many cars and buses, and I knew I needed to find a place I could sit down, and maybe eat.

"In my hometown, you could go to a café and sit for hours without ordering. I thought I could do that here too. So I went to a café down the street. I sat in a seat. When the waiter asked me what I was ordering and found out that I had no money, he told me I could not stay there. It was the same in most places. So I finally started looking at the trash cans for food. It is easiest when you follow someone and they throw out what they don't want to eat, because then it is still fresh."

Jenice cast her eyes down.

"It is shameful to eat trash and steal, but I have nowhere else to go."

Katie hugged her again. "There is absolutely no shame in fighting to survive, Jenice. And that is what you have had to do."

Katie looked to Aliyah. "This place her momma is at. It sounds like one of those detention centers, right?"

Aliyah nodded. "I've counseled a few who have managed to get out of those places. They're horrible. I'm not surprised she told her to run."

"What do we do now?" Katie looked to her friend.

"Well, for now, I told Jenice she could choose to leave whenever she wanted. So I think the decision lies with her."

The women both looked at Jenice, who was staring wide-eyed and wet-faced at both of them.

"Jenice, remember I said you could leave whenever you want. Our lunch is finished now. Do you feel like leaving?"

Jenice, shocked, responded, "No! No, please don't leave me alone!"

Katie, yet again, hugged Jenice fiercely. "We will not leave you. You will not be alone again." She pulled back and looked intensely at Jenice. "Okay?"

Jenice nodded meekly.

"We will figure out how to help you." Katie hugged her again fiercely.

Aliyah put her hands on both of them and said, "Yes. We will figure out how to help you."

For the first time in months, Jenice breathed a sigh of relief.

Chapter Eleven

Sarah

Three-year-old Sarah and the other children stared as their mother threw the one pot they owned on the floor in a fit of rage.

"Just stop! I can'a do this anymore!"

It was a daily scene in the small shack they all called home. Jane, who was six years old and the oldest of the five children, stood up from the floor in her tattered and torn dress and picked up the baby, who had been crying for hours with no break, from the makeshift cradle her father had built. Sarah watched her sister try to soothe the baby as she had seen her father do many times. The baby began to calm a bit.

"Fine thing, tha'. She'll stop her caterwauling fer you and your Da, but fer me she jus' wails an' wails!" Her mother, Lillian, continued smashing about the tiny spot in the shack that they called a kitchen. As she turned to face the stove again, Lillian tripped over her two-year-old son, Leo, who had crawled closer to the stove to get warm.

"Jesus, Mary, and Joseph! Leo Edward Smith, ya ge' ou' of my way or I'll knock ya to next Tuesday!"

The two-year-old began to cry loudly as his mother nudged him harshly to the side.

"That man. Knockin' me up and then havin' the nerve to lose his job while we go' five mouths to feed." Lillian continued to mutter as she began to cook what meager goods they managed to get their hands on that day. "If 'e comes at me again, I'll kick 'im where it counts. No more children on my watch! I didn't even want 'em in the first place. But what's a woman's role, but to lie down and take it and then do all the child rearin' an' heavy liftin.'"

She looked out to her children and shouted, "I was goin'ta be a famous actress! Then you lot came an' ruined it fer me!"

Suddenly Lillian stopped her monologue and took a step back and started to cry, her head in her hands. Sarah, scared and confused, looked to her sister Jane, the eldest, who was still holding the infant, who hadn't even been named yet; Leo, two years old, and cute as can be, was crawling toward his brother James, five years old, who didn't seem to know what to do either.

"Sarah, sweetheart, will ya sing me a li'l tune?" Lillian begged of her three-year-old.

Sarah, who had been cowering in silence by the little table that barely fit three of them, brightened a bit and nodded her head. "Yes, Momma." She began to sing "Ring Around the Rosie." Sarah was already well-spoken because she loved to sing so much.

Lillian set her spoon down and sighed. Then she started to tap her foot to the beat. The children all looked at her, unsure what to do.

"Well what're ya waitin' fer? Dance!"

They all smiled and got up to form a circle. Jane placed the baby beneath a blanket full of holes in the makeshift cradle their Da had made out of scrap they had scavenged outside. They grabbed hands and sashayed around the tiny room as they giggled and took up the words to the song. Even Lillian joined them. For a brief moment in time, mother and children were at peace with each other.

A loud noise at the door stopped the entertainment. Thomas Finnigan was standing at the door, sopping wet from the cold rain that was quickly turning to snow outside.

He held up a slip of paper.

"No jobs to be had in steelwork, m'dear! But they pay soldiers!"

"No! No, Thomas Finnigan, you din't?"

"Oh, I did, m'dear. T'aint nothin' to be had out in this harsh town. It was that or keep starvin' an I won't stoop so low as to not be able to feed my li'l uns. They were goin' t' grab me up any day now anyway with the draft startin'."

"A bit late for that sir," Lillian said with a scowl that could burn holes in a man's face.

Thomas's face hardened for a moment and then relaxed again. It made Sarah shake for a moment as she watched her Da look at her Ma.

"Now, Lily, y'know I've tried. It's tough times, and the way they treat t' workers a' those steel mills, it's downright un-human. At least if I die in war, I'll die havin' done somethin' I'm proud to be a part of."

Lillian welled up with tears and collapsed into Thomas. It made Sarah want to cry, too.

"I can'a! Thomas, I just can'a be left alone w't all these li'l uns! It's all I can do to make it through!"

"Lillian, the army is payin' two shillings a day. I know it's not as much as steel, but steel jobs ain't existin' right now. No jobs are. It's bet'a than nothin'."

Lillian pushed away from Thomas and stared out the window, a far-away look in her eyes. Sarah, even at three years old, knew her mother wanted to be somewhere else, performing, although Sarah didn't really know what "performing" was. Still, she heard her Ma talk about it often. That she was trapped by their Da and she should have had a different life. Sarah didn't understand. Her father was always nice and gentle with her and her siblings, and with her mother. She didn't understand why her Ma wanted to go away from them.

Jane stood up and said, "Ma, I can help take care of 'em."

Thomas and Lillian both looked sad when Sarah's sister said this. Times were forcing children to grow up too soon, and this family was no exception. Thomas's face looked weary as he said, "Yes, Jane, th't would be a big help while I'm gone." He wrapped his oldest child in a hug and Sarah ran over to both of them and was enveloped in the group hug. "I'm afraid you children will have to pitch in and take care of each other and more of the household tasks while yer mother finds some par'time work t' help with the daily costs." Thomas looked pointedly at Lillian, who had started at the mention of her. Sarah pulled away from the hug in time to see her mother's face grow angry. It made her cower back toward the table.

"Fine t'ing tha'. I believe I've done more than my fair share o' the work around 'ere wha' with almos' dyin' from three o' their five births!" She motioned to all the children, and they all put their eyes down.

Thomas stood and tried to gently pull Lillian into a hug, but Lillian pulled away. Sarah saw her father's face harden.

"Now Lily, I know ye've had a hard time of it these pas' few years, but . . ."

Lillian whipped around to face Thomas, rage in her face.

"A hard time? How could ya ever know tha'? Ya don' know the half of it. You're the reason I'm 'ere! You an' yer charm and promises. I never shoulda said yes to ya that night after my show! But ya wore me down! Ya kept showin' up and I could'na say no! Ya said things would get bet'a and I could keep performin'—the only performin' I done since I metcha was between the sheets! Yer a rascal! And ya can'a keep a job te save yer life! You've ruined any chance a' me ever being anyone a' impor'ence! Now I'm just 'ere lookin' after the children ya insisted we keep havin'! Now I'm jus' a mother an' a wife, two things I never planned te be! Ya go aroun' sayin' yer lookin fer work an' I know that ain't the truth. Ya coulda got'ten work easy enough pickin' up trash, but that's no' good enough fer ya, is it?"

Thomas looked stricken. Sarah was now huddled with her siblings, shaking as her mother continued her rant.

"Yeah I know you had the oppertuni'y and ye didn't take it." Lillian looked absolutely terrifying to three-year-old Sarah, eyes afire, pointing a ragged finger at her father. "An' now ye expect me te take care of yer *five* children while ya go off an' play soldier an' likely get killed!"

At those words, Sarah started to cry. "Are ye goin' ta die, Da?" the sweet child asked.

Thomas looking angrily at Lillian, turned to Sarah, knelt, and took her in his arms. "No m'darlin'. Yer Da is just goin' to help this country win this war. I'll be back before ye know it. And ye won't be alone. Ye can ask the neighbors fer help as ye have before. And ye can lean on each other." Thomas dried Sarah's tears and hugged her tight. Sarah could hear his heart beat then feel him take a deep breath. She watched her mother from his lap. Lillian was collapsed on the stool at the small table they ate their meals. She seemed to be sobbing into her arms with her head on the table.

"Lily, sweet'eart, it's only temporary." Thomas brought Lillian out of her meltdown and was met with a deep scowl.

"'at's what you always say." Lillian stood and picked up the pot, setting it on the tiny stove. Sarah brightened, hoping it meant she was calm again and would be making food soon. Her tummy rumbled.

"They're sayin' t' war'll only last a l'il bit an' then I'll be back wit' bet'a credentials havin' worked so hard in the army, ya see. They'll be clamberin' to give me work after tha'," Thomas answered.

The cry of the baby interrupted the argument.

"She's 'ungry again, Ma," Jane picked up the infant and brought her to her mother. Lillian gave a huge sigh and glared at Thomas before taking the baby and attaching it to her breast.

"She's 'ungry. He's 'ungry. We're all 'ungry. Seems like it's all I do is be feedin' the lot or lookin' for food to feed ya," Lillian reiterated.

"Well tonight, I'll be feedin' the lot!" Thomas pulled out a small ham and some potatoes, not nearly enough to feed all the mouths present, but it was more than they'd had in days. The children gathered around. Sarah's tummy grumbled loudly again. Lillian stayed back with the baby.

"Now what'd ya have to do to get tha'?" she accused.

"Never you mind, missus. I thought we should have a fine feast on my last night 'ere with ya." The children giggled with excitement.

"Ya mean to tell me yer leavin' tomorra?" Sarah heard her mother's voice tremble. Thomas set down the food and wrapped his arms around Lillian.

Softly he said, "Now Lily, they've got ta train me before they let me loose on the enemy. I head out to Durham for trainin' early in the mornin'."

Sarah watched her mother turn into her father for a moment while she cried. Lillian's tears stained Thomas's shirt while he comforted her. For a minute, Sarah felt happy to see her parents showing such affection. But then, Lillian pulled away angrily and turned to the small stove and began the process of boiling water for the potatoes. The moment was gone. Sarah didn't understand. She just wanted her mother and father to be happy.

Thomas turned back to the anxious children and put on a smile.

"Now, when I came in, I heard someone was singin'?"

"Me, Da!" Sarah wiggled with excitement.

"Well get on yer way then, li'l one! How abou' 'London Bridge'?"

Sarah smiled and began to sing the well-known children's song. The others set out the meager place settings they'd managed to scrounge up around the neighborhood: mismatched plates, only three spoons to share between them, forks with missing tines, a large but rusted cutting knife, and glasses that Thomas had carved from wood. The little ones sat on the floor while Thomas took one of the chairs and sat Sarah on his lap as she continued to sing. He leaned in and whispered to her:

"My li'l songbird. Yer singin' is like angels' wings. Keep singin', my li'l darlin', and know I'll be back as soon as I can."

Sarah turned and leaned into her father as she finished the last verse.

Chapter Twelve

Katie

"Seven . . . six . . . you're coming back up the stairs from your happy place. Five . . . four . . . soon you'll be present again. Three . . . begin to stretch your arms and legs. Two . . . one . . . Open your eyes, Katie. You are safe and you are here."

Katie opened her eyes, warmth surrounding her, a blanket over her legs while she lay on the couch in the hypnotherapist's office.

That was amazing.

She turned her head to look at Aliyah's colleague, Janet Everwood, world-renowned hypnotherapist and Eastern medicine guru. A soft light illuminated her, creating an aura around her head. Beautiful pastels hung on the wall of all different shapes and sizes. A bookshelf stood tall, full of titles from the doctor's trade as well as various crystals. A gorgeous lavender curtain draped over the window to block out any harsh light. The couch Katie was lying on was a soft gray, and the blanket was another hue of light purple. Everything about the office was inviting, as if saying "Come here to relax and heal."

"How do you feel?" Janet said with compassion.

"I feel . . . I feel relieved. Lighter, somehow. Like I finally know what's going on."

"You took quite a trip into your past lives just now. I recorded three: Sarah, Anya, and Roseamund."

"Roseamund. I had never dreamt of her life before today, but I know I lived it. I felt it."

"Sometimes people are unaware of the number of past lives they have lived until they start doing these sessions. Normally those lives are where some of the deepest pains existed and therefore the present mind chooses to block them out until the individual is ready to deal with that pain."

Katie raised her eyebrows and blinked several times. This was all just so . . . insane. But it wasn't. She knew it wasn't. She *had* lived those lives. She thought those thoughts and experienced those events and emotions.

"Tell me more about your moments with your Council. Can you describe what you saw, what you heard. Some of the things you said during the session were that the Council was feminine and appeared as a wall of flames with circular shapes within each flame, almost like faces. Were you afraid of this Council?"

"No. The opposite. I felt loved and supported. Like they were all motherlike figures with caring, strength, and understanding. Guiding me to understand myself and why things happened. The lead Council woman, uh, flame, had a deep, resonant, calming voice. She helped me see that much of my journey in these lives has been tied to children. That I seek the love of a child."

"You mentioned there were others not of the Council present during these moments in front of the flames. Do you know who they were? Often, when you feel the presence of other entities that are not your Council, they are other spirits who have traveled multiple lives with you and are deeply connected to you."

"Kind of like soulmates?"

"Well, in a way, I guess you could say that. Yes, kind of like soulmates. Do you know who they were? Is there someone in your current life who reminds you of these entities?"

"Yes, I know exactly who they were: Aliyah, my current life best friend, and Chad, my fiancé. Chad was standing next to me on my right, his head turned to look at me, but with his body kind of in a protective stance facing the flames. Aliyah was diagonal to me on my left, facing me with her right hand on my shoulder. They were not in human form per se, just more like bodies of light. Aliyah's felt so comforting, and Chad's just felt so supportive. I feel like maybe Aliyah's spirit has been with me from the start of my journey and Chad for at least the last two."

"That's wonderful, Katie. Wonderful work. These two are most certainly your linked souls, or soulmates, if you want to call it that. Each entity often has a protector and a mothering entity that they travel through the various lives with. It sounds like Chad is your protector and Aliyah is your mothering influence."

Katie laughed. "I could have told you that without this session!"

Janet smiled warmly. "Yes, we often have an instinct that we've known people before. You've heard the phrases 'They're an old soul' and 'I feel like I've known them for a lifetime already'?"

Katie nodded.

"Well, that is your inner spirit nudging you to remember the connections with spirits you've been connected to in previous lives."

Katie shook her head slightly. "I'm sorry, this is just all so . . . wild. I mean, I feel it's true, but it's just . . ."

"Out there?" Janet smiled again.

Katie breathed a sigh of relief and laughed again. "Yes. Sorry. It's just a lot to wrap my head around."

Janet nodded. "Which is why we only do these sessions a few times. Once the portal is opened to the Council in the present life, often no additional sessions are needed because they will start sending you messages directly. Many clients find that, after one session, they start receiving the answers they are seeking pretty quickly."

"You said each soul often has a mothering influence and a protector. I know I've been the mothering influence, but could I be the protector too?" Katie asked.

"It's quite possible you could be both, even in one life, for another soul, yes."

Katie's mind reeled from the information and experience she had just had. Past lives. Multiple past lives. A protector in the form of her fiancé and her best friend, a motherlike influencer. A Council of flame, guiding her every move in each life. It all made sense. It was completely insane, but it all made sense.

"I think that's enough for today's session." Janet moved to her desk and opened what looked like a schedule book. "Would you like to schedule another one to possibly explore some of these lives further? Perhaps Roseamund? Or we can wait a little bit and see what answers may come to you and then go from there."

"I think I would like to schedule another one, but maybe if things come to me before then, we can change what we plan to do?" Katie answered.

"Of course. Past life work is very fluid. We try to go with where the Universe is leading us in these sessions. How about one month from now, and you can call me if anything changes?"

"One month from today, same time works for me. Thank you, Doctor."

Janet gently placed her hand on Katie's shoulder and smiled. "Please, call me Janet."

Katie smiled gratefully back. "Can I give you a hug? I haven't felt this . . . I guess relieved or hopeful . . . in a long time, and it's thanks to you."

Janet laughed, "Of course! I'm a hugger, too."

They embraced and Katie, for the first time in months, felt a warm glow and a calm come over her. It was like her mother was hugging her. She hadn't realized how much she had desperately been seeking this. Even if things changed and they didn't end up having that second session, Janet was another spirit connection she wouldn't soon forget.

Katie pulled back from the hug and gathered her purse. As she walked out of the office, she turned back to Janet, "Thank you. You've helped more than you could know."

Janet smiled warmly, "You're welcome."

Katie closed the door on her way out and began the short walk to her car.

Three lives! And Chad and Aliyah have been with me through most of them.

The thoughts circled in Katie's head as she got into her car and started the engine.

I need to write this down before I forget it.

She pulled out of her parking space and decided to head for the café. She knew she needed to get it all onto paper before too long.

And Roseamund. Who is she?

Chapter Thirteen

Roseamund

It was a beautiful day. The sun was shining so much that the manor house was practically glowing through the paned windows. Roseamund did not notice. She did not feel the warmth of the sun on her skin nor see the light trickling through her bedroom window. She lay motionless, skirts up to her neck, as the Lord of the Manor crawled off her and buckled his pants. Her face stung from the slap he'd given her as she'd tried to refuse him this time. The pain this man, her father, if she could even call him that, had given her after so many years of this had taken its toll. She felt empty, torn, ripped from any semblance of a life she once dreamed of living as a small child.

"Pull your skirts down girl. You look like a whore," Lord Giovanni Devaro, or the Lord Tyrant, as many called him in the shadows of the manor house, gruffly said as he left the room.

Roseamund lay there for a few more minutes until she was sure he was gone. Slowly she sat up and smoothed her skirts down. She stood, walked to the table by the window, and reached beneath it. She pulled out a small shard of a looking glass she had hidden in the crevice under the table. It had been her mother's. The only remnant left that she could remember her by. She stared at the bruise beginning to form under her eye.

"Mother, I cannot do this anymore. How did you survive it for so long?"

Roseamund set the mirror down and sighed. *She didn't survive it,* a voice in her head said.

Roseamund was the bastard child of the very same Lord who had just left her bedroom. The only reason he allowed her to stay in his house at all was because he desired her so much. Her mother had been an indentured servant in the manor house, and the lord had treated her much the same as he now treated Roseamund.

Until one day, her mother decided to fight back.

She had used the looking glass, a piece of which Roseamund had just been holding, to stab the lord in an attempt to disable him in order to get away. While it had injured him enough to cause a permanent limp, her mother's attempt to get away had failed. The lord in his anger had her remanded by his guards and brought to the top of the manor house. He had gathered all who lived and worked there in the lawn below the front of the house to watch as he told them all what a low-life whore her mother was and that she had committed treason within the house, attempting to murder him. He then shoved her off the roof. She fell to her death in front of everyone, including little three-year-old Roseamund.

Roseamund shook her head as she tried to forget the flashback. Since then, Lord Tyrant had ravaged a level of tyranny on the household that no one, not even his wife, Lady Arabella, could stop.

Lady Arabella had always been a balm of sorts for the lord. Her soft and steady voice could calm an angry sea. Often after his tantrums, the houseworkers could hear her quietly speaking to him, telling him how he was right, to placate him, and to try and ignore whatever issue was causing him ire. Many knew their marriage had been arranged and that this was likely her only way to survive the waves of his narcissism and rage. However, to the rest of the house she would show small kindnesses when she could. An extra piece of bread to the starving servant girl in the kitchen; a believable excuse to the Lord Tyrant when his head horse master snuck away to be with his wife, who was having a difficult birth. The house knew she had a kind heart, but she had to build walls around it and rarely show it in order to stay in Lord Tyrant's good graces and not become a victim to his wrath, as well.

One point of contention between the couple was the fact that she struggled to bear children, a burden that Lady Arabella and Roseamund both shared. Roseamund deep down inside knew she was unable to bear children. The number of times she had been with Lord Tyrant without any pregnancies, plus her age, proved that she was barren. She knew it would only be a matter of time before Lord Tyrant began to shun her because of a lack of children. Roseamund knew Lady Arabella feared the same, with three miscarriages, one stillbirth, and no heirs to present. With every lack of child, the Lord Tyrant would rape more and more of his servants. He had so many bastard children, they had lost count. One could see the devastation in Lady Arabella's eyes as she walked around the manor. Once a beautiful young woman, the pain and abuse had taken their toll on her appearance, and she now wandered the halls as a shell of herself. The two women shared the same pain.

It was an existence that Roseamund had always lived, never knowing a life without trauma. However, she did know love. Her mother had taught her that love, above all else, was to be cherished and given as often as possible, no matter the circumstances.

With these thoughts in mind, Roseamund left the room to begin her daily duties as the kitchen assistant, a job she actually enjoyed.

Cook had been hard at work for an hour already when Roseamund arrived at the kitchen. She didn't yell at her, however. It was common knowledge what Lord Tyrant did to any woman under the age of twenty-five, and one that would get a severe lashing if spoken of. So Cook just nodded to Roseamund and said, "We'll be needing potatoes today. You can go to the fields on your own. Gwendolyn has been delayed. I'll send her to meet you when she gets here."

The two shared a knowing look, and Roseamund picked up a large basket and headed out the door toward the potato field.

As she was walking the path that took her to the field, she finally noticed how bright the sun was. Almost as if the sun were trying to cover up any darkness that spread through the manor. She hummed the beginning of a tune her mother used to sing to her:

> *And the lass leapt to her lover's arms*
> *Free at last to love . . .*
> *Free at last to live.*

A scream tore through the lands, like a knife to Roseamund's heart. It was little Gwendolyn; there was no doubt. Roseamund only hesitated for an instant before dropping her basket and running toward the sound.

What Roseamund found when she got to the location of the screams was horrifying. They were in the stable—Gwendolyn, Lord Tyrant, and Gwendolyn's mother, Marie. It was clear that Roseamund's guess as to why Gwendolyn had been delayed to her kitchen duties was correct: Gwendolyn's dress was covered in dirt and hay and bruises were forming on her arms from Lord Tyrant's large, strong hands holding her down. She stood by the edge of the stall he'd pinned her in, shaking, hugging herself, trying to comfort herself, tears streaming down her face as she released a guttural cry of grief. What had caused the child to cry out was also clear: Marie lay motionless on the ground, a pitchfork gutting her to the ground. Lord Tyrant, cleaning his hands of what could only be Marie's blood with a dirty stable cloth, stood over her, sneering, a dark rumble of a laugh beginning to come up from the depths of his evil soul.

"Shut it!" he growled at Gwendolyn. "The wench had it coming. How dare she try to interfere with me!" He spat on Marie, turned to leave, and noticed Roseamund standing there. He walked up to her and threw the cloth in her face.

"Clean up this mess and shut that child up or so help me god she will go the same path as her mother."

He left the stable, grumbling to himself as he went.

Roseamund flew to Marie's listless body. She grabbed her hand. Still warm.

"Marie? Marie!"

Marie fluttered her eyes open. She stared at Roseamund for a moment, looking confused. Then she looked to her daughter.

"Gwen." It was a faint whisper, but Gwendolyn dropped to her mother's side and grabbed her mother's other hand.

"Momma, I'm here. I'm here." Gwendolyn sobbed softly.

Marie moved her gaze back to Roseamund, now looking resolute.

"Save her."

With those final words, Marie breathed her last breath. Her gaze went dull. She was gone. Gwendolyn fell upon her as her cries ripped from her.

Roseamund's hand gripped Marie's and she began to shake. As the anger coursed through her, she leaned down to Marie's ear and whispered, "I will. I will save them all."

Chapter Fourteen

Katie

Katie woke to Chad shaking her.

"Katie! Katie, honey, wake up!"

She opened her eyes and saw panic in his.

"Wha-what?"

"You were screaming in your sleep. So loud I was worried the neighbors were going to call the cops! Are you okay? What in the hell were you dreaming about?"

Katie took a moment to come out of her stupor. She thought about what she'd just witnessed in her dream—no, experienced. She didn't think she could feel any worse than she had when she'd miscarried her child, but this, what Roseamund had endured, was a contender. She felt abused, abandoned, and angry all at once. She looked up at Chad and burst into tears. He gathered her in his arms and held her as she cried.

"Sweetheart, you have to talk to me at some point. Please. Please, talk to me."

His request was so gentle, pleading in a way, that Katie knew she couldn't hide these dreams from him any longer. No matter his response, she had to share with him.

She sat up, sighed, and looked him in the eye.

"What I am going to tell you is probably going to sound crazy, but please hear me out."

Chad hesitantly nodded. "Okay."

"I've been having dreams . . . about my past lives."

"Your past . . ." He looked a bit incredulous.

"Please, you said you'd listen."

"Alright. You've been dreaming about your past lives. How do you know they are past lives?"

"I just do. There's a feeling, a knowing, that I've *lived* these lives. I'm not usually observing in the dreams—I *am* the woman in the dreams. I feel what she is feeling, see through her eyes, know her thoughts. They are like memories, not dreams. I know what's going to happen next, as if I'm reliving a movie that I starred in."

Chad took a moment to let it sink in. He looked confused, but then shook his head and said, "Go on."

"As you know I've been having these dreams a lot since we lost . . . since I miscarried."

Chad nodded and reached for Katie's hand. She pulled it away, hesitated, then put it back, letting him comfort her.

"Well what I haven't told you is that one of these dreams I've had, exactly the same each time until a few weeks ago, since I was little. Honestly, since before I can remember."

"Wow, Katie. Why didn't you share that with me if it's been going on for so long?"

"It's not something I am proud of. Honestly, I was ashamed of it. I thought if I told anyone about it, they'd have me committed." She laughed softly at the statement. How different things were now.

"Honey, I love you. I would never do that. You have to know that, right?"

He looked at her imploringly, a hint of uncertainty in his eyes.

"Yes. I know that. It had nothing to do with you. It was all *my* insecurities."

"But you're one of the most confident people I've ever met!"

"On the outside. I'm really good at pretending and acting professional. I'm also really good at hiding my feelings."

"I'm beginning to realize that."

"It's not fair to you."

"You know you can always tell me anything, Katie. I will always try to listen and help you if I can. I just wish you could trust me about this."

"I do, Chad. I'm sorry I haven't. Again, nothing to do with you. It's all me."

Chad looked at Katie for a long moment.

"Maybe you should talk to someone, like a professional, about all of this. I am here, and I will listen, but I don't know exactly how to help you and it's all I want to do."

Katie smiled. He was truly her soulmate, and she knew it. Always her protector.

"I already have started to see someone."

Chad looked surprised but stayed silent.

"She's a psychologist and past life regression hypnotherapist."

"A past what?"

She laughed.

"Past life regression hypnotherapist. Basically she hypnotizes you and helps guide you through any past lives you've lived in order to find answers to what lessons you may be needing to still learn in your current life."

Chad took it all in, then shrugged.

"Okay. So did you find your answers?"

"Well, I discovered that my affinity to loving all things Renaissance era were because I actually lived in the Renaissance era in Italy. That life is a more recent revelation. Like literally the dream you just woke me from. You know I've always felt connected to that time period,"

Chad nodded.

"It's because I was there. In a lord's manor house. The bastard child of the Lord Tyrant who raped me on a regular basis and killed my mother in front of me."

"Whoa, what? Your father raped you and killed your mother? That's so, so dark and wrong, Katie!"

"Yes, but I know it happened. And he did it to almost all of his female servants. He had so many bastard children that no one knew how many he actually had. He was a monster of the worst kind, bringing terror to everyone who crossed his path. I don't know because I woke up before I could learn this, but I have a feeling that I did something to help save those women and children."

Chad just sat for a moment looking stunned. Katie could tell he was trying his hardest to really process what she had just told him.

He shook his head for a moment, as if clearing his thoughts, then said, "Okay, so you had a really bad life during the Renaissance era. You mentioned other lives? What was that one you have been dreaming about since you were little?"

"My dream has always been about my death. It is the 1960s. Now I know it was 1961, to be exact. I am in a powder blue party dress, and I am a professional singer on the way to a gig. It is night on a back country road, and it's raining. A man is cradling my head in his lap as I begin to slip away. I always just heard his voice vaguely, never able to make out what he was saying, and I always see a bright light. I know I'm bleeding from my stomach and my head. He's crying. Then I die."

"Jesus, Katie."

"I know."

"And you've dreamt this since you were little? That's pretty heavy for a five-year-old to handle."

"It is. I just never knew how to tell anyone about it."

"Did this therapy session help you figure out what happened and why?"

"To an extent, yes. I learned that my four siblings and I had been abandoned by my mother when my father had to go to war. We were extremely poor, and I think now she was likely suffering from postpartum depression and just couldn't handle being on her own with five children living in a shack in England."

"So instead she just left her five children to fend for themselves in a shack?!"

Chad was visibly angered by this. Katie's heart felt warmed by his reaction, knowing he would never let a child suffer like that.

"She did. And what led to my car accident was that Sarah, the woman I was, had seen her mother in a diner after not seeing her for years. I wanted to go in and ask her why she'd abandoned us, but something held me back. There was a sense of understanding and shame that I still don't get that caused me to not go into that diner and question my mother. Then later, as I was driving in the rain, I was so engrossed in my thoughts about my mother that I just lost track of where I was. I drove onto the wrong side of the road and there was a truck coming the opposite direction. It hit me head on and I was thrown from the vehicle."

"Holy shit."

"That's where the dream had always picked up, just after that moment."

"Katie, wow. I just, I . . . I don't know what to think about all of this." Chad took another moment, then asked, "You said you had three lives? What was the other one?"

"A female tribal leader and healer named Anya who lived in 210 B.C. and led her people through the freezing Bering Strait to get to warmer climates. The tribe lost several of their warriors on the journey, and she felt the weight of those deaths as they settled into their new life in basically what's Alaska today."

"Wait, 210 B.C.? As in thousands of years ago?"

"Yes. My visions with this life start as she is trying to save the life of a young girl whose father was one of the warriors who died. I am struggling to save her until I realize she is literally dying of a broken heart."

They sat in silence side by side, still in the spots they woke up in on their bed, for several minutes. Katie turned to face Chad again.

"Say something," Katie implored. Chad turned toward Katie and leaned into her, a look of worried hesitation on his handsome face. He gently tucked a piece of hair behind her ear, a caress he often used as a show of affection.

"I . . . I guess I just don't know what to say after all that. It's a lot, Katie. I can't believe you've been having to carry this all on your own, on top of losing Joshua."

A look of immediate regret came over his face as Katie quickly pulled away from him.

"Katie, I'm sorry, I'm so sorry. I didn't mean to say his name. I know how much it hurts."

She looked at Chad—this man who'd been by her side through it all, many times not understanding how she felt or knowing what to do, but still staying with her. They had both gone through the death of their child. She realized he'd been grieving, too.

"No, I'm sorry, Chad. For closing you off and not sharing in our grief together. This past year must have been so hard for you. I'm so, so sorry."

She leaned into him again, tears falling down her face. They embraced.

"I lost you for a while. It was so hard to lose the baby, but then I lost you too and I didn't know how to get you back." His gentle words stung Katie, but she leaned into him further, trying to comfort him.

They held each other for what felt like hours.

"I think you should take a leave of absence from your column."

Katie pulled back, startled.

"What?"

"I know you've been struggling to write them. Sam called and told me he was worried about you. That you've been late with assignments and what you do turn in is a half version of what he knows you can write."

Katie grew angry. "He had no right!"

She stood up from the bed and started pacing the length of the wall next to the bed. All the fears of losing her job because of her lack of effort these past few months came flooding into her head at once.

"Sam's worried about you because he cares, Katie. He thinks you are one of the most talented writers he has ever come across, and I have to agree with him."

"Really?" This stopped Katie short. Sam, the head of the biggest newspaper in Arizona, thought she was one of the most talented writers he'd come across?

She shook her head. She sat back down on the corner of the bed, placing her hand on Chad's leg gently.

"I can't just stop the column. We need the money."

"We will be okay." Chad sat up and placed his hand on hers. She could see a proud glint in his eye. "I'm up for a promotion at work. I think I'm going to get it, too."

She'd been spending so much time wrapped up in her own issues that Katie realized she hadn't even noticed or thought to ask how work was going for Chad. He was a brilliant lawyer and worked so hard to get to where he was in his firm. She felt embarrassed. She moved closer to him and placed her hand on his chest.

"I'm so sorry, Chad. I haven't even thought to ask. That's so amazing. I'm so proud of you. "

"It's okay, sweetie. It also means you can take a leave of absence and focus on you and healing for a while. Maybe you should think about writing about all these lives you've lived."

Katie thought for a moment, looking out the window at the world passing her by outside. *Maybe I should.*

"Chad, there is something else I need to tell you."

He looked a little wary.

"It's not that I was the guy who hurt you in one of your lives, is it?"

She laughed.

"No. No, in fact, you are my protector soul."

He took that in for a moment.

"You mean I've had past lives, too?"

"Yes, we've been together for a long time, you and me. Aliyah, too."

"Wow. This stuff is blowing my mind. Maybe I should go get some past life therapy."

"Maybe."

"Was that the something else you needed to tell me?"

"Not exactly." She paused, contemplating whether she wanted to go ahead with it or not. She decided yes.

"I met a little girl who is unhoused. She's a runaway from the detention centers. She was separated from her mother, who is still in the detention center and set to be deported if we don't do something. The little girl's name is Jenice. She's been on her own for months. She's only nine! Aliyah and I finally were able to get her to trust us and we gave her lunch and learned about what she'd been going through. Aliyah has worked with the state to secure her as a foster ward of the state for now. She needs a home where she can stay and feel safe while they try to figure out what to do with her. I want us to take her in!"

Now it was Chad's turn to look stunned. He leaned back against the headboard again and ran his hand through his chestnut blonde hair before he dropped it into his lap.

"I . . . don't know what to say."

Desperate for a yes, Katie pulled herself closer to Chad and faced him directly. She grabbed his hands in hers.

"Please, Chad! Please, I need this. I know this is what I need to help me heal. And her, too. I feel a deep connection with her, and I just know we need to help her."

"Yeah, but taking in a child we don't even know, who may not be with us for very long . . ."

Frustrated, Katie dropped his hands and stood again. This time she paced the whole frame of the bedroom. She threw her arms out beside her. "That's the whole point of fostering!"

Chad stood up, too, and halted her pacing, placing his hands on either side of her. "Yes, I know, sweetie, but do you think it's really the best thing to take in a child that you might have to give up? We just lost Joshua."

Katie looked at Chad, tears in her eyes.

"Please, Chad, I need this. Yes, yes, I think it is the best thing for me and for her. I have to save her."

Chapter Fifteen

Katie

"So you've been a healer in 210 B.C., who saved her whole village; a woman in fifteenth-century Italy who is the victim of multiple traumas including incest, who plans to save all the women and children living at her manor house; a singer in the 1940s and '50s who was abandoned by her mother, raises her siblings basically on her own, and then dies in a car crash after seeing her mother again? Damn girl, that's a lot. Like a lot a lot." Aliyah looked incredulously at her best friend. The patrons of the café bustled around them, the mid-morning light casting rays of sunlight on various spots on the ground around them. The women didn't notice, too involved in their conversation.

Katie nodded and sipped her coffee. Aliyah shook her head, "Well no wonder you want to take in Jenice now. Sounds like you've been saving kids for a long time."

Katie looked up sharply.

"I never thought of it that way. You're right, Al. I have been saving, and losing, kids for a long time."

Aliyah's eyes saddened. She leaned forward in the overstuffed, brick-red chair, reaching for her friend's hand. "Oh honey, I didn't mean it that way—"

"No, I'm not hurt. It's the truth. I haven't told you everything that happened yet."

Aliyah stopped her hand mid-reach. "Okay . . ."

Katie looked nervous. "I've been getting more flashbacks of my lives, not just in dreams now."

Aliyah leaned back into the chair again, thoughtful. The barista shouted out a name in his loud, nasally voice behind her. They both glanced over at him with annoyance before turning back to each other.

"Like a triggered memory? My trauma patients often have those. They come more frequently as the brain decides it is okay to let them remember. Normally it means they are ready to deal with the trauma. This is fascinating!" Aliyah said. She took a sip from her tea, obviously eager to hear more. "Okay, go on." She waved at Katie to continue.

"Well, Sarah had a child. A boy."

"And . . ." The concern on Aliyah's face grew as Katie fought back tears.

"And . . . she abandons him." Katie couldn't even look at her best friend. The shame she felt from this life she didn't realize she'd lived was overwhelming.

Aliyah sat up straighter and set her tea down on the brown, glass-topped side table next to her. "Wait, what? How do you know?"

"He's not with me at the end of that life. For the last few days of that life, he's not there. I had all these flashes of being pregnant with him, playing with him, holding him. Then, he's not there anymore. I think that's why I was so distracted when I hit the truck and why I had that understanding about my mom when I saw her through the diner window." Katie felt absolutely distraught.

Aliyah leaned into Katie and grabbed her arm across the side table in a firm, supportive way. She tried to catch Katie's eye, but Katie wouldn't look up at her. "Okay, but that doesn't mean you abandoned him! Maybe he's visiting with his grandpa or one of your siblings because you had all those singing gigs—"

"No, no." Tears welled up in Katie's eyes as she finally did look at Aliyah. "There is a deep sadness in me when I die in that life. I know I've left him. Just like my mother left us."

Aliyah squeezed Katie's arm compassionately, then leaned back into her chair again and picked up her mug. She blew out a big sigh. "Wow. Katie, this is so much."

They sat in silence for a few minutes, sipping their drinks—tea for Aliyah, hot chocolate for Katie. The barista called out another nasally name and it broke them out of their thoughts. Then Aliyah looked at Katie.

"Maybe something happened. Like what's happened with Jenice and her mother. Maybe you were forced to separate from him. From what you told me about Sarah and all she did for her siblings before and after they were reunited with their father, I just don't see her leaving her own child."

Katie sadly smiled at her friend. "Maybe that's the reason she does leave him, because she never had her own life. Because she had to be the mother and the martyr from a young age after her mother left them. Maybe she was more like her mother than she knew. Maybe she just wanted to live a life free of responsibility for once."

The thought hung in the air for a moment, like a dark fog, sucking the marrow out of the room.

Aliyah fiercely shook her head. "No. I just don't think so, Katie. There's got to be more to it. Maybe you should talk with Janet about it."

"Mind reader." Katie gave a half smile. "I already have an appointment. I need to get to the bottom of this."

Aliyah reached out and squeezed Katie's arm again, this time enthusiastically.

"That's my girl! There's more to it. I know it."

Katie looked out the window at the people passing by on the street. So many untold stories. She set her hot chocolate down on the table, then looked to Aliyah intently.

"There's more to all of them. I intend to find out everything. And then I intend to write about it."

"Like a book?" Aliyah looked surprised.

"Yes, a book. My story, their stories. I think it might help a lot of people."

"What about your column?"

"I'm going to talk to Sam after this. Ask for a leave of absence. Chad and I talked. He's up for a promotion at work and he thinks it would be good for me to take some time to process losing . . . to process the loss and sort through all of what's going on with me." Katie looked down at her hands, gripped them tight as she tried to hold back more tears.

"You know it's okay to say his name," Aliyah said gently.

Katie looked up at Aliyah, whose face could not have been more compassionate. Katie released the grasp of her hands and looked away from her friend again, to the world outside. A whisper escaped her.

"I know. I just . . . I guess I feel like if I don't say his name, then maybe it didn't happen."

After a moment, Katie turned back to look at Aliyah and could tell she was being analyzed.

"Just say it."

"Whether you say his name or don't, Katie, it will not change that it happened. That your son died and there was nothing you could have done to prevent or change that. Maybe saying his name will help you begin the process of acceptance and true healing."

Annoyed, Katie gathered her purse and jacket off the chair, wanting to get away from the conversation. "Okay, Dr. Jones. Thanks for the analysis."

Aliyah grabbed her arm before she could make her escape, though, and Katie reluctantly sat back down.

"No, Katie, I don't mean to analyze. This is just me, your best friend, trying to help because I am concerned about you. I see your pain and I just want to help."

Katie sighed, looking down at her hands again. "Chad said the same thing."

"He's not wrong."

Katie looked up to see her friend, staring intently at her. Not even her best friend understood what she was going through, but she knew her heart was in the right place. Katie backed away from her annoyance and softened a little. She set her jacket and purse back down on the arm of the chair.

"I know, I know. I just need to go through this in my own way. That's why I think he's right about taking a leave of absence. I'm not focused on my column. I've been turning in half-assed assignments for months. Hell, the other day I completely forgot a deadline. Sam has been far more understanding of all of this than any editor should be."

"He cares about you, too, Katie. We all do."

"No, I know. I just cannot be a burden to anyone anymore. Writing is always how I've processed things. So taking the time to write through everything that's going on . . . I think that's the way I'm going to start feeling better."

Aliyah paused for a moment, sipped her tea, took a bite of her salad, and studied Katie again.

"You're doing it again." Katie laughed.

"Sorry! I apparently can't help analyzing, even when I'm trying not to." Aliyah laughed, too.

Katie shared a genuine smile with her friend, reached over, and grabbed Aliyah's hand, giving it a squeeze. "It's why you're the best at what you do."

Aliyah squeezed back. "And you're the best at what you do, Katie, but I get it." She let go of Katie's hand and waved hers in the air. "Sometimes you just have to let go of things to really get a handle on them."

"Spoken like a professional!"

Katie and Aliyah laughed again. The annoying barista called out another name, clearly pronouncing it incorrectly, and the women fell into an even bigger fit of giggles. Katie was grateful; it had been a while since she had laughed. The giggle fit subsided and the two sat in silence again for a moment, just smiling at each other, a lifetime of memories connecting them in comfort.

"Anyway." Katie's eyes dropped to her hands, interrupting the moment. She was rubbing one thumb over the other, a comforting movement she'd performed as long as she could remember to help ease her anxiety.

Aliyah smiled.

"She's okay, Katie. She's at the girls' home for children waiting to be rehomed with foster parents."

Katie looked up again. It was as if her best friend could read her mind. Then she found herself saying, "I want to be that foster parent."

Again, the statement hung in the air.

"Katie . . . do you really think that's a good idea? With all the things you're processing. Bringing a child into your home—"

"Is how we can both heal!"

Aliyah looked stricken.

"I'm sorry," Katie said quickly. "I didn't mean to snap. I just—I just think that I can really help her, you know?"

Aliyah sat silent for a moment.

Aliyah looked serious. "Katie, fostering is not adopting."

"I know!" Katie hit the arm of her chair with her hand in frustration. The anger behind the movement shocked them both a little. She took a breath. "I know. I've thought a lot about this. If I cannot have a child of my own, I want to be able to help the children that already live on this Earth. I want the opportunity to be a mother, whatever that looks like, even if just for a little bit. I need to do this!"

"You will likely have to let her go at some point—"

"But for the time I have her, she will know love instead of the pain she is experiencing right now!" Katie wanted nothing more than to get up and start pacing, but the crowded café kept her from doing so.

"Even when you are caring for her, you won't be able to shield her from all pain, Katie." Aliyah kept her voice calm. Katie knew she was trying to speak reason to her.

"I know! But I can love her through it!" Tears were streaming down Katie's face now. She could feel the tension between her and her best friend. She didn't care. She needed Aliyah to understand.

"You'd be okay with giving her back to her mother if we can get that to happen? Or letting her go if the state decides to deport her with her mother back to Mexico?"

"I will fight tooth and nail to make sure *neither* of them gets deported! And yes, I would gladly give her back to her mother, because I know what it feels like to lose that connection! I would never stand in the way of that bond. But maybe, just maybe, I can give that little girl the sliver of hope she needs to keep going until the day when she can be reunited with her mother." Katie didn't even realize she was speaking through gritted teeth. Other customers were beginning to stare at Katie with concern on their faces.

"Breathe, Katie. Take a breath." Aliyah spoke very slowly and very calmly. She gently put her hand on top of Katie's balled fists. "Just breathe."

Katie took a breath and looked around her. Everyone in the café had stopped what they were doing and were staring at the two women having a very heated conversation in the middle of the restaurant. Some whispered and leaned into each other. The annoying barista looked especially disgruntled.

Katie sat down, only just then realizing she was standing. She looked around at everyone.

"I'm sorry. I'm sorry, everybody." Embarrassed, she sat back down.

The regular hustle and bustle of the people around her resumed, as if nothing had happened. Katie couldn't bring herself to look Aliyah in the eye.

"I need this. I need to do this."

Aliyah lay her other hand on top of the one already holding Katie's hands.

"Katie . . ." the tone in Aliyah's voice caused Katie to slowly look up. "I know. I'll put in a call."

The relief that flooded through Katie was palpable. Aliyah wiped the tears from her friend's face.

"You always were an ugly crier."

It was enough to break the tension, and both women burst into laughter. Katie paused long enough to say, "Thank you."

Chapter Sixteen

Jenice

Jenice opened her eyes and looked around. For a moment, she forgot where she was and anticipated having to get up and move quickly before anyone yelled at her to move, which so often happened when she slept on the park benches or in the street alleys. But then she realized she wasn't outside.

She felt the warmth of the blanket on top of her, the firmness of the mattress beneath her. A soft pillow cushioned her head—a far cry from the newspaper roll she usually used as a pillow. Slowly, she began to take in her surroundings. She could hear the quiet breathing of the other girls in the room. There were eight to a room, sleeping in bunk beds. She had one of the bottom bunks. She had always wanted bunk beds. She used to beg her momma for them. Now she would never mention them again if only it meant she could see momma again. Tears stung her eyes, and she blinked several times to make them stop. She wiped away a stray tear that had managed to escape and sniffled.

"Hey! You okay?"

A whisper from the bed next to her startled her. She looked quickly to see who was talking. It was a young girl who looked a lot like her: brown eyes, dark brown hair, but maybe just a bit older. "It's okay. You're safe. They're really nice here." The young girl gave Jenice an encouraging smile. Jenice faintly smiled back.

"I'm Bianca. What's your name?"

"Jenice."

"Be quiet!" An annoyed grunt from one of the upper bunks stopped the conversation.

Both girls looked at each other and quietly giggled.

"See you at breakfast," Bianca mouthed.

Jenice nodded and waved. She lay her head back down, waiting for the morning bell to signal it was okay to get up, looking forward to breakfast for the first time in a while.

The dining room was large with white walls and sterile rectangular tables and metal chairs. The girls in the group home could sit where they like as long as they did not cause any trouble.

Jenice had just picked up her tray of food—eggs with ham slices, a scoop of fruit, and milk—and was scanning the room, hoping to see Bianca. The room was full of sound: clanking silverware, noises coming from the cooking in the kitchen, and so many children's voices chattering.

"Boo!"

Jenice jumped and nearly dropped her tray as Bianca snuck up behind her. Bianca was wearing a bright pink T-shirt that said *Don't Worry, Be Happy* in yellow. There was a beautiful white daisy at the end of the phrase.

"Oh, sorry! I'm sorry. I didn't mean to really scare you." Bianca looked earnestly at Jenice. "I bet you're still jumpy cause you just got here."

Jenice's shoulders relaxed a bit, and she nodded and smiled slightly. She looked down at her own ragged, faded blue shirt with nothing on it, and her smile dropped from her face. She looked back up at Bianca with sadness in her eyes. Her momma had bought her that shirt.

"It's okay! We all were kinda that way when we first got here."

"How long have you been here?" Jenice asked with a new curiosity.

"About six months," Bianca quipped as she started off toward an empty table.

Jenice's eyes widened. *Six months? I can't be here six months. I need to find my momma.*

"But a lot of girls are only here for a few days before they go into their foster homes," Bianca added quickly, obviously noticing Jenice's trepidation. "I'm just here because my foster home was real bad and they thought I might do better with more structure."

They set their trays down on the white laminate table and sat across from each other.

Bianca dug into her eggs like she hadn't eaten in days. Jenice just watched her, hesitant to try the food in front of her even though her tummy grumbled.

"Why was your foster home bad?"

Without even looking up, Bianca responded between bites: "Oh, the dad was really mean. He'd hit everyone in the house a lot. He liked to scream at us and would lock us in the basement when we did stuff he didn't like. Sometimes we'd be down there for days with no food or water."

Jenice looked terrified.

"Where was the mom? Why didn't she protect you?"

"She left a while ago I guess, but they didn't tell the social worker. He'd always tell the lady that she was grocery shopping or something like that anytime there was a visit." Bianca had finished her eggs and was moving onto her fruit.

"How did you get out?" Jenice was so enthralled with Bianca's story, she forgot she was hungry until her tummy let out a loud rumble. She glanced around the room to make sure no one heard, then picked up her fork and took a small bite of ham. It was the best-tasting thing she'd had in weeks. She closed her eyes for a moment, reveling in the salty good-ness. Bianca's response brought her back to the stark room.

"One of the kids broke the basement window and crawled through it and ran to the neighbor's house to call 9-1-1. He had a bunch of cuts on him so the neighbor believed him. The cops came and rescued us and arrested Gary. I think he's in jail now or something."

Jenice breathed a sigh of relief. "That's good."

She picked up her fork again and took a large bite of eggs. They tasted okay, not like the food at the café where she met Katie, but they were okay. Jenice set her fork down and fell into thought. Katie was so nice, and Aliyah. She wished she could see them again.

"Hey! Hello? Earth to Jenice!" Bianca was waving a hand in front of Jenice's face. Jenice snapped back to the present.

"Where'd you go? You know they only give us thirty minutes to eat. If you're hungry, you better get going!"

Jenice nodded, looked around at the other children, and realized they were almost all finished eating. She glanced down at her almost-full plate and started eating again.

"So what about you? Did your foster parents suck, too?"

Jenice shook her head with a mouthful of fruit.

"Nof, Im wz pff ina dttn sstr an rn awa," Jenice said.

Bianca laughed out loud. "You were what? Puffed in a downtown sister?"

Jenice swallowed and began to laugh, too. It was the first time she'd laughed in a very long time.

"No, I was put in a detention center and ran away!" She kept giggling, but Bianca quieted down.

"You mean one of those ICE detention centers? For immigrants?"

Jenice stopped laughing, suddenly sad, and nodded.

"My momma and me traveled a really long way. She kept saying we were going to seek asylum in America. Our guide left us right before the border, and we were grabbed by scary men right when we crossed it."

Jenice paused for a second, realizing several of the girls at their table had also quieted down and were listening to what she was saying. They all had fearful or sad looks on their faces. Jenice took a deep breath and continued.

"They took us in a truck to a big building. Two bad men opened the truck. My momma kept saying, 'Asylum! Asylum!' but they wouldn't listen. The scary men grabbed me and my momma and one started pulling her away to a different vehicle. She was screaming, 'No! No! Asylum,' but they just kept pulling her. The bad man held me so tight I could barely breathe. Momma told me to run, but he wouldn't put me down. I just watched Momma be taken away as he carried me further from her. He took me to a little room inside a building. I could hear kids down the hall crying. I was so scared."

Bianca and the other girls at their table had been listening intently, totally silent, looks of pity and terror on their faces.

Bianca whispered, "How did you get out?"

Jenice looked around at all the girls, expectantly waiting to hear how she escaped. She took another deep breath, the memory fresh in her mind, and continued.

"I did what Momma told me. I ran. I was sitting in that little room where the bad man told me to wait while he made a phone call in an office next door. There was a door at the end of the hall and a guard next to it. Then there was a loud noise, like people fighting, and the guard ran out the door. It didn't close all the way. So I just got up and ran. No one saw me because there were people fighting outside. There were trees really close by so I ran into the trees and just kept running. Then I got to a street with a lot of people. I got scared, so I stayed in a lane between buildings until night. There was some cardboard by a trashcan in the lane. I think it's called an alley? I slept on the cardboard. Like we used to at home."

"Where is home?" Bianca quietly asked.

"El Salvador." Jenice teared up as she remembered home. It was scary and dangerous, but she had her momma then and felt safe with her there, which was more than she could say now.

"My momma and papa came from Mexico," Bianca sadly said.

Jenice's eyes lit up. "You're not an American?"

Bianca shook her head. Some of the other girls joined her shaking their heads, too. For the first time, Jenice really took in who was sitting at her table. So many of the girls had her skin color, her eye color, her hair color. She realized she wasn't alone in her story. Bianca's response brought Jenice's eyes back to her new friend.

"I was two years old when they crossed the border. My papa got caught, but he got me and my momma on a truck before it happened. They were supposed to bring us to safety."

Tears slid down Bianca's cheeks.

"What happened?" Jenice asked, her food forgotten.

"The truck crashed. Everyone inside it died, except me. They found me on the side of the road. I got taken on as a ward of the state and put into foster care. That's how I ended up with Gary and finally here."

The gravity of both of their stories settled over all the girls at the table like a weighted blanked. Some of them were crying, too. The connection they shared was something they wouldn't fully comprehend for many years, all of them being so young, but Jenice felt especially connected to Bianca, her kindness and positivity shining through even the darkest of times. They were being forced to grow up too fast and endure hardships no child should ever have to. Bianca and Jenice looked each other in the eyes, both full of tears.

"These eggs suck," Jenice said to break the silence. Bianca's face split into a smile and they both broke into fits of giggles, joined by a few of the girls around them, ending the shared painful moment with an understanding that this was their life now.

The bell signaling the end of breakfast rang, and the two little girls jumped up from the table and took their trays to the trash bin.

"What happens now?" Jenice asked Bianca.

"The best part of the day—recess!" Bianca grabbed Jenice's hand, and they ran out of the dining room to the world outside.

Chapter Seventeen

Anya

"Be careful, child!" Anya chastised as she stopped Yaari's hand from dropping some leaves into the concoction in front of them.

They were circled around a large cauldron sitting atop a firepit in the center of Anya's hut. Steam was pouring out through the hole at the top of the hut's sloped ceiling. There were bowls of herbs, spices, and flowers on the wooden counter next to them. Yaari's hands were stained a light yellow from the turmeric she had dropped into the potion in front of them, just before the last ingredient attempt. Anya was sitting on a hand-carved stool given to her by the village woodcarver, resting her tired feet. She had spent the morning scavenging for the flowers they were using now. The stool had little symbols up the legs, each one representing a protecting or healing spirit.

"I thought astragalus was a part of the potion?" Yaari's frustrated response caused Anya to laugh lightly.

"Only if you want to make everyone run to the trees and relieve themselves in an unfortunate manner."

Yaari only continued to look confused and frustrated. She put one yellowed hand on her hip, staining the brown tunic she wore, and her other hand to her forehead, trying to remember what Anya had told her before they began. Yellow fingerprints shown on the spots where she placed her hand to her face.

"But you said, to lesson the inflammation, one parts ginger, two parts licorice root, one part fennel, a pinch of elderberry, and two parts ast . . ." Yaari paused at Anya's lifted gaze. "Oh, not astragalus! Oregano! Two parts oregano." She threw her hands down by her sides in fists, then took a deep breath and relaxed her hands.

"I'm so sorry, Mother Anya, I didn't remember."

Yaari's defeated gaze prompted Anya to stand up, walk to her, and take Yaari's hand in hers, speaking gently, "It's quite alright, child. You are learning. You will soon know all there is to know, even more than me, I'm guessing." Anya smiled and patted Yaari's hand reassuringly.

"Do you really think I'll be as good as you someday?" The child, now looking more like a young woman every day, asked earnestly as she pinched two parts oregano into the cauldron and began to stir the remedy.

"I know you will. Better even, I believe."

Yaari stopped stirring for a moment, looking forlorn. Her eyes held a far-off gaze, and the muscles between her eyes created two worry lines. Anya recognized that look; Yaari was remembering their long journey through the ice and snow to get to where they were now, remembering how her father and many warriors could not fight the ice and froze to death.

"I don't know if I can lead like you, Mother Anya. You are so strong. You don't question yourself. I always question myself!"

It was Anya's turn to gaze into the past, remembering how she felt when she could not battle the elements to save her people. She could only pray to Mother Earth and Father Sky, asking them to help her guide those who were left to safety. It was the only time in her life as tribe leader and healer where she could not use her gifts to protect everyone, and it rocked her to her core.

"My child, not true. There was a time when I lost my confidence, where I questioned whether I was fit to be a leader for this tribe anymore."

"When?" Yaari looked incredulously at Anya.

Anya gave Yaari a bittersweet smile.

"When I had to save you, Yaari. Your father was lost, as were many of the tribesmen, and we were losing you, too. I had managed to bring the village to safety from the elements, but I could not figure out how to save you. I thought you were going to leave us, but then I felt your strong spirit and knew you would fight if I could just give you a lifeline."

Anya gestured to the herbs and spices on the countertop, the lifelines that had saved Yaari those few years ago.

Yaari stepped close to Anya and put her hands on her shoulders, looking into her eyes with deep gratitude. She was now as tall as Anya.

"And you did. You saved me, Mother Anya."

For a moment, Anya accepted the thanks, but only for a moment. She broke Yaari's gaze and turned back to the wooden counter covered with herbs. She began to put away the herbs that were no longer needed.

"No, you grabbed the lifeline and saved yourself, young one. And you will do the same for many others."

Anya knew her time as healer and leader was coming close to an end. How long she had, she didn't know, but she would make sure Yaari knew everything she needed to before that time came. Just as Anya had learned from her mentor that healing is part knowledge of herbs and spices and how they go together, but also part knowing and following her instinct, Yaari would do the same.

I must teach her to trust herself. To know she is capable of great things. To use this gift to help others even when she does not think it will.

Yaari began to help Anya put away the unneeded ingredients, hanging the dried basil back on the wooden post of herbs holding up the ceiling, dropping the elderberries back into their storage container made of clay. Anya stirred the tincture they had created, smelling it to make sure it was the right potency.

"This is an excellent mixture, Yaari. You created just the right ratio. It will help many people with the insect bites they've been experiencing."

Yaari beamed and walked back to the counter to peer into the cauldron.

"You really think so? I know it's just for bug bites, but it's the first one I've made on my own! Well, almost on my own." Her eyes cast downward, clearly embarrassed at the memory slip she'd had earlier.

Anya cupped Yaari's face between her hands. She knew her hands were warm but rough, weathered by years of picking the ingredients that now filled her hut. A healer's hands, full of power, grace, and love. Yaari leaned into the embrace.

"You did excellent, young one. You only have to trust your instinct and intuition."

A commotion at the front of Anya's hut interrupted the moment. Two warriors came through the doorway, one half carried by the other. The sick warrior's skin was a pale shade of gray except where the bites on his skin looked more like angry welts, swollen with pus and ooze. Anya could immediately tell he was burning with fever by the redness in his cheeks and pallor of his eyes. He had a wild look, as if he were seeing demons fly around the hut. He wheezed several times and then vomited in front of the women. The warrior holding him upright winced, looking slightly disgusted, but did not let his friend go.

"Mother Anya! Please, please help him!" Amaruq, the healthy warrior, sounded panicked, his voice strained.

"How long has he been like this? I just saw him yesterday to treat his bites."

Anya calmly approached the warriors. Tulok, the sickly one, was unaware of his surroundings. His eyes were rolling to and fro, and he was moaning, clearly hallucinating. She placed her hands on his forehead; it was burning.

"Quickly, Amaruq, bring him to the pallet."

Amaruq half dragged, half carried Tulok to the pallet bed on the floor in the corner of the hut and dropped him slowly onto it. Tulok's moans grew louder. He turned to his side, clearly in pain, and vomited again.

"Yaari, the tincture. A full bowl please. And a clean rag."

Anya inspected the bites on Tulok's arm. They were obviously infected, but she knew it was something more. These insects had transferred some kind of illness into this man. What it was, she did not know; she had never seen insects like these before moving to this land. It was yet another obstacle that she knew her village was about to face.

"Mother Anya?" Yaari was standing next to Anya, a clay bowl of the tincture they had made in one hand and two clean rags in the other. Anya looked up and noticed the fear in Yaari's eyes. She could see it in Amaruq's, as well. Whatever fear or doubts she was feeling, she knew she must take control of the situation and remain calm. She gave Yaari a reassuring smile.

"Here child, come sit on the other side of Tulok and help me cover these bites."

Anya took the bowl from Yaari and placed it within reach of both of them, near Tulok's head. She accepted one of the rags and dipped it into the bowl before dabbing it on the harshest-looking bites. Tulok let out a cry. Amaruq winced again at his friend's pain.

Yaari had already settled herself on the other side of the ill warrior and repeated Anya's motions, dabbing the infected areas.

"Amaruq, over in the corner there, you will see a deep brown flask with a dark stopper. Please bring it to me. It will help slow the fever."

Relieved at being given instructions, Amaruq walked to the other side of the hut and located the flask. He grabbed it gruffly and quickly brought it back to Anya. She lay her rag down, accepted the flask, and removed the stopper. She glanced at Tulok, who was writhing in his pain, and looked up to Amaruq.

"I need you to hold his head still as I pour in the liquid. We do not want him to choke, and he is not fully with us right now."

Amaruq nodded, knelt down by his warrior brother, and grasped Tulok's head in his hands, attempting to hold him as still as possible. Anya pried Tulok's mouth open and held his chin while she slowly poured drops of the medicine into his mouth. At first he fought it and began to choke.

"Sit him up slightly!" Anya's direction was sharp.

Amaruq lifted his friend's head and shoulders into his lap, holding the sides of Tulok's face firm as Anya continued to pour in additional drops of the dark liquid. Tulok stopped resisting and seemed to enter some sort of trance.

"Good. It is working. His fever will break soon. Now we must heal these infected bites." Anya floated her hands slowly over Tulok's body and closed her eyes.

The infection is systemic. There also seems to be a virus, a flu. This must have come from the insects. His spirit is strong, though. If we move quickly, he will survive.

Anya breathed an audible sigh of relief and opened her eyes. Yaari was watching her, concern in her eyes.

"Mother Anya?"

"His spirit is strong. He will need a lifeline. Yaari." Anya motioned to Yaari to inspect the patient herself.

Yaari looked stunned and a little trepidatious but also excited. This was her first time diagnosing a real person.

"Trust yourself, my child. Use your hands, feel the energy. Close your eyes and listen with your heart. What is Tulok's body telling you?"

Yaari gazed one second longer at Anya before taking a deep breath and closing her eyes. She slowly began to take inventory of Tulok's energy with her hands.

Anya's attention moved between Yaari and Amaruq, who was watching Yaari silently as she worked. He had a look of respect and reverence as he gazed at the young healer. Anya could tell he sensed the strong energy coming from Yaari. It was the same power that emulated from Anya.

"His fever will break soon," Yaari said aloud as she continued to scan. Anya nodded silently. "The infection from the bites has filled his entire body; it is systemic. But there is another entity, a virus of some kind." Yaari tilted her head, eyes still closed, as she tried to listen to what her intuition was telling her. "An influenza." She opened her eyes and her hands snapped back to her side as she looked quickly at Anya.

"Am I right? A virus coming from the insects?"

Anya gave a small smile of pride, but there was gravity in her voice.

"Yes, child, you are right. We must warn the village."

Chapter Seventeen

Sarah

Sarah sat on the floor looking up at her mother as Lillian looked at her five children's faces.

"Now don'cha be lookin' at me tha' way! I done all I can fer ya' and this is the only way. I'll be ba' in a few days. Jane, you've got enough food fer t' week an then I'll bring som'more."

Sarah could see her sister Jane, now eight, stare at her mother angrily. Sarah stared, too, frightened. How long would she be gone this time? Last time it was ten days before she came back. Jane and James had to go seeking food scraps on the street while Sarah, only five, had to watch her younger siblings Leo, four, and baby Grace, now two. They had not seen their father for that year and a half; he had been sent to the front lines shortly after his initial training. They had nearly frozen to death, as the winter had been harsh and they often ran out of fuel for the small wood-burning stove in the shack.

"I'll be ba' soon. I jus' need a li'l break." The tone in Lillian's voice sounded to Sarah like it would be a long while before she saw her mother again. Lillian gave each child a hug. She lingered with Sarah and whispered in her ear, "Don'cha ever let someone trap ya. You go' a gift and it's meant to be shared. Take care o' yer sisters an' brothers, li'l one. I'll see ya again."

Lillian stepped back from the favored child, wiped away a frivolous tear, and waved to them all faintly as she walked out the door. After that day, most of them never saw her again.

It was months since her mother had left, and Sarah, now five years old, was nervous. The streets were exploding with voices and shouts. People were running through the streets, waving their arms, kissing, hugging.

Sarah peered out through a crack in the shack's front door, curious as to what all the chaos was about. Was it another bomb threat? The sirens weren't going off, and it didn't seem like people were scared.

"Victory! Victory! We've won! The Nazis have surrendered!"

The Nazis have surrendered? While her five-year-old mind didn't quite comprehend the meaning of this statement, she did know that the Nazis were the bad guys and that if people were jumping up and down and smiling, shouting this from the streets, this must be a good thing. She turned back to her little brother and sister and smiled.

"The Nazis 'ave surrendered!"

Leo looked at her quizzically and Grace smiled back, babbling as little ones do when someone smiles at them.

"Nazis?" Leo asked.

"The ba' ones!" Sarah began to dance around the little room, grabbing up her brother's and sister's gaunt hands and circling and singing, like they'd done with their mother.

> *London bridge is falling down,*
> *falling down, falling down*
> *London bridge is falling down*
> *My fair ladies.*

They all fell down in a giggling heap on the floor. It was their favorite game to play. However, they stayed down, as the exertion for all three had tired them tremendously. These past months with their mother gone had been very hard on all the children. They were malnourished and all battling skin issues due to lack of hygiene, even though Jane tried to make sure everyone washed when they could.

Poor Jane and Jack had become the parents for the little brood. They often were out scavenging or begging in the streets while Sarah watched the little ones at home. Sarah did what she could to keep the younger two entertained. She loved having siblings and enjoyed the play they did every day, but it was getting harder and harder to enjoy anything the longer they were abandoned.

For all five, nighttime was the worst. It was when they missed their parents the most. They would lay on the makeshift mattress, made from straw and cotton scraps and set on the floor, and huddle together to keep warm. Often, they could hear crying or fighting outside their walls, as was customary in the area where they lived. A few times, a man who'd had too much drink—the children had nicknamed him Sloshed Sal— would wander by muttering to himself. One time, he tried to enter their shack and they had to all sit against the door to keep him from pushing himself in. James kept shouting "This is na' yer house mister!" Sarah thought he sounded terrified but protective at the same time. Eventually the man gave up and went on his way.

One of the few things that brought the group some joy was when Sarah sang.

Jane and Jack would trudge in after a long day of looking for food. Sometimes they'd have something, sometimes they wouldn't. But every time, they would sit down around the little table and Sarah would go stand by the stove. She'd sing every nursery rhyme she knew, and when she ran out, she'd even make up her own songs. Some melodies were upbeat and raucous and would urge the children to clap or sing along, and some were full of melancholy and were haunting, bringing the children to tears. They all missed their mother in their own ways, but their father was the one they missed the most. He had been gone fighting for nearly two years. He would write every once in a while. Sarah's songs and those letters were what kept them going.

One day a letter arrived from Thomas, and in it contained the words they were all hoping for:

> *My dearest little ones and Lily,*
> *The war is over! They are sending us home. I'll be there soon.*
> *Look for me in a few weeks.*
> *With all my love,*
> *Da*

When Jane read the letter in halting stutters to everyone, as she had only just learned her letters from a kind woman living down the lane, a cheer went up in the room. Their father was coming home! Finally, the drudgery would end!

But a week went by. And then two. By the third week, the children had given up hope that they would be reunited with their father. At this point, they had all started scavenging for food on the streets, as their little tummies would not let them just sit at home and do nothing. Sarah always had little Grace with her, and frequently Leo would lag behind her a few paces.

During one of these scavenger hunts, little Grace collapsed. She had been acting ill for a day or so. Sarah had fallen to the ground, too, the weight of her sister yanking her down with her too much for the rail-thin girl to withstand. Leo ran up, "Wha' happened?"

Sarah looked at her baby sister, who was red in the face and crying. She felt her cheeks and realized that Grace's skin was on fire.

"I think she's sick. She's burning. Feel." She grabbed her brother's hand and placed it on Grace's cheek. Leo yanked it back quickly.

"Don't! She might give it t' us!"

"She's burnin' up, Leo! What do we do?"

"I dunno. Let's find Jane and James. They'll know wha'ta do."

Leo waited as Sarah picked herself up and then picked up and carried Grace, who was half her size. The trio began to slowly make their way down the lane. The streets were crowded, as Sunday was almost upon them and everyone was out shopping, purchasing the last supplies they could for their gatherings. The children could smell the chicken cooking in the nearby café and their stomachs flipped. Sarah was so hungry and dehydrated at this point that it nearly drove her to do something she knew she would regret, like stealing a little bit of the roast leftover by a customer on the café table close to them. Leo sniffed and stared longingly at the meat. He went to reach for it, but before he could, Sarah began to sing.

> *Here we go round the mulberry bush,*
> *The mulberry bush,*
> *The mulberry bush.*
> *Here we go round the mulberry bush*
> *On a cold and frosty morning.*

It was Leo's favorite song and one she sang often to distract him from getting into trouble. It worked. Leo dropped his thieving hand and began to sing along with Sarah. They sang all the verses; it was how they had both learned to clean themselves, taught to them by their mother, one of the few gifts she left them. As they sang, they stopped intermittently to call out for Jane or James.

"Jane!" Sarah cried heartily.

"Jamesey!" Leo shouted his brother's nickname.

They continued with the song verses between shouts. Sarah had to stop several times, as little Grace was too heavy for her to carry for long. But the poor baby was delirious with fever and couldn't walk on her own. They ended up dropping her between the two of them—Leo holding her up on one side, Sarah on the other—and partly dragging her, partly lifting her as they continued their macabre chanting down the road.

The people around them did not take notice. They'd seen children like these many a time: street rats who were up to no good, always looking to splinch your wallet and such. How mistaken those people were. If only they'd taken a moment to notice how young they were, to ask if they needed help, they would have discovered the truth. But to the crowd, these children were invisible.

It was on the fourth verse of "Here We Go Round the Mulberry Bush," the one about brushing teeth, when Sarah heard a voice say her name. One she had not heard in a while. It was music to her ears, more beautiful than the voice that carried melodious tunes out of her own mouth.

"Sarah? Sarah! Sweet'art! Sarah my darlin'!"

Her father, Thomas Finnigan, was standing only a few feet away from them, a frantic look in his eyes. She couldn't move. It was such a beautiful sight. She was rooted to the ground, holding up her baby sister next to her. Leo dropped Grace's arm and ran to his father.

"Da!"

Thomas leaned down, scooped up his boy, and gave a relieved and hearty laugh that was also filled with tears.

"Leo! Oh, Leo, m'a boy! Thank the Lord! Thank the LORD!"

Thomas hugged him as if it were the last time he would see him. They were both crying.

"Da, we thought we'd never see ya again!"

Thomas gave him another firm squeeze and set him on the ground. He looked to Sarah and Grace. Sarah realized he was staring at them with horror. She looked down, ashamed. She knew they all looked thin and dirty, as if they'd not bathed for months. But she had tried so hard to care for her younger siblings while her older ones searched for food. She glanced up to her father again with trepidation, not knowing if he would yell at her for doing such a poor job like her mother sometimes did. She flinched back as her father gently approached with a sad yet angry look on his face. She felt silent tears pouring down her face. She clung to her baby sister as if protecting her from a monster.

"Sarah?" he said gently. "Sarah, it's your Da. You recognize me, dont'cha?" He softly reached to help her with baby Grace, but she wouldn't let him touch her. She glared at him, a flash of anger and what looked like despair and mistrust in her eyes.

"Sarah, it's alright. I'm here. I'm no' leavin' again, I can promise ya tha'. Here, let me help you with the baby." He reached again for Grace, and this time Sarah let him take her, the burden being too heavy for her to continue to carry. The moment the baby was out of her arms, she let out a wail and threw herself into her father's grasp.

"Oh, Da! It's been 'orrible! Just awful! We waited an' waited for ya, but you kept not comin'! We were so 'ungry, we just had to ge' out and ge' food. Jane and James 'ave tried so 'ard to take care of us, but they's only lit'l like us! I kept singin' tryin' to help us feel be'a, but it's been so 'ard without Momma! We been lookin' an' lookin' for ya. 'ow did ya find us?"

Sarah watched as her father's face went from confusion, to anger, to resolute.

"I found ya from yer singin', lit'l angel. Yer angelic voice led me right to ya. I couldn'a mistaken it for anyone else's. You could bring world peace with tha' voice." Thomas meant it. Sarah's sweet little voice was something that had gotten him through his darkest days of combat. "Ya said yer mother isn' with ya. Where is she, lass?"

Sarah became quiet for a moment.

"She wen' to find work, Da."

"An' when was that, lit'l one?"

Sarah shook her head. She didn't quite know, as she hadn't learned how to keep track of time yet.

"I' was four months ago, Da." The voice came from behind them. It was Jane's. Sarah could feel her father go still for a moment before he turned to look at Jane.

"My dear, brave Jane. Where have you been?"

"We were out looking for food. Then we heard Sarah and Leo calling for us and singing. When the singing stopped, we thought something might be wrong and we came running as fast as we could to where we'd heard the sound before. Oh Da! It's been so long! It's been 'orrible! I tried so hard to make sure we were all fed, but without Ma, i' just got harder!" Sarah saw the tears running down her older sibling's faces and it made her cry even more.

Their father's silence was deafening. His hands shook as he quietly asked the group, "An' what did yer Ma say when she left ya?"

Sarah saw the look in Jane's eye, the nod that urged her to be the one to speak up. Then she looked up at her father, fearful. She didn't want to get her mother in trouble; she still loved her in her own childlike way, but she knew she had to tell him.

"She said 'I jus' need a li'l break.'" Sarah cast her eyes downward.

Jane stepped forward, "She also told Sarah to no' let anyone trap her. That she got a gif' 'at needs to be shared. An' she does, but I don' think it's fair she only told 'er tha.'"

Sarah looked at her sister, stung. She didn't know Jane had heard what her mother said to her. She loved her siblings with all her little heart could muster. There was no ill intent or malice within her. She believed they all held different gifts that had helped each other make it through these hard times. It was their closeness that she cherished most. Her sister's words stung her. It was the first time in her young life she'd experienced what jealousy from another could feel like. She didn't like it.

"I didn't know she'd do tha'!" Sarah broke into tears again and stamped her foot, then threw herself into her father's arms, sobbing.

"Shh. Shh, li'l one. Of course you di'n know. Yer mother has put all a you in a right spot. There is no blame to be placed among ya."

Thomas hugged Sarah fiercely and gathered the others in his arms, as well.

"This was my faul'. Yer mother was never fit t' be a mother, a' leas' not t' so many. I love children and always wan'ed a big family, but I didna think about the toll i' would take on 'er. I don' blame 'er for bein' upset. Bu' I will never forgive her fer leavin' ya."

He pulled back and Sarah watched him look each child in the face. The look on his face made her think he must have felt what she did earlier, sad and ashamed. She heard him blow out a harsh breath.

"Can' ye forgive yer Da? I'm sorry, my loves, I'm ever so sorry. I promise, you will never have t' go hungry again."

Tears streamed down everyone's faces, even baby Grace. Jane nodded, Sarah hugged her Da harder, Leo looked at his Da with love in his eyes. James took a step back from them, looked hard at his father for a moment, then softened his gaze and put his hand upon his father's shoulder and said, "We can fergive ye, Da. Please don' ever leave us again."

Thomas pulled his son into a firm embrace. Sarah heard him whisper fiercely in James's ear.

"You've been forced t' grow into a young man before yer time. I will never forive m'self for lettin' tha' happen, but I will work t' make it right."

They pulled back from each other and all sighed with relief. For the first time in months, they all had brighter looks on their faces. Sarah was even smiling.

It was baby Grace's wail that broke their reverie.

Thomas looked down at the two-year-old in his arms. She was flush with fever, and the dehydration was prevalent in her dry, cracked lips.

"Oh my child! I've led you to this illness an' I don' even know what t' call ye!"

Jane interjected, "Grace. 'er name's Grace."

Thomas looked at his baby girl once more.

"Grace. Shh l'il one. We'll ge' you bet'a quick as can be." He looked up at his children and stood, holding baby Grace tight.

"Come. Is the Mission House still standin'?"

James nodded. "It took a small hi' when the bombs came, but yea, it's still there. They been 'th ones who been checkin' in on us sometimes. We didna wanna be sen' t' the work 'ouses so we always jus' said momma was lookin' fer work, even after we knew she wasn'."

The look on her father's face made Sarah think he had just been slapped. But then she saw him take another breath, shake is head, and square his shoulders. "Lead the way, ma boy."

Chapter Eighteen

Roseamund

It had been days since Marie's murder. Roseamund had been the one to make sure she'd had a proper burial, in a field under a tree, far away from the manor house that had taken her life. She planted poppies, beautiful orange and white poppies, all over the grave. The house servants, those who could sneak away, held a small service at the gravesite in the middle of the night while Lord Tyrant was sleeping. At the end of the service, Gwendolyn lay next to her mother's grave, crying inconsolably. Roseamund, who was trying not to cry herself—because she knew if the tears began to flow, they would never stop—knelt next to the young girl and gently placed her hands on either of the girl's shoulders.

"Come, Gwen. She's gone to a better place. No amount of crying you do here will be able to bring her back. Come with me, and let's get you a warm blanket next to the fire."

She coaxed the girl to her feet, Gwen's sobs wracking her little body, as they began to shuffle away. Roseamund knew Gwen's life would never be the same. *When you witness your mother die in front of you, you are changed forever*, she thought as they made their way across the field. *When you witness your mother murdered in front of you, it changes your soul.* Rosamunde squeezed Gwen closer to her. *I will always protect, you little one.* Gwen looked up into Roseamund's face, as if she knew her thoughts. She leaned her head onto Roseamund's shoulders, and the tears began to dry.

As they turned to walk toward the manor house, a flash of something behind one of the trees caught Roseamund's eye. A figure was standing in the shadows. The person motioned to Roseamund to come to them.

Roseamund turned to one of her fellow servants. It was Cook.

"Please make sure Gwendolyn gets to bed. Make sure she is warm and someone stays with her. I'll be along shortly to relieve them of their duty."

Cook nodded. "I'll make her a drought of tea." She gently took the child under her arm and led her away from the field.

Roseamund turned her attention to the figure in the trees. As she quickly strode to where the person was standing, she wondered who it might be. Was the flash from a sword of one of Lord Tyrant's loyal spies? The thought sent shivers through her. If tonight was her time to die, she'd be ready to fight, or run, if needed.

As she drew closer to the figure, she could see the person was petite and had a large cloak with a fur hood covering their head. There was only one person who owned a cloak such as that. Lady Arabella. Roseamund stopped short for a moment. A sword-wielding spy she could take, but the wife of the man who raped and killed half the manor house, including her mother? She was not sure how to deal with that. She began to step one foot in front of the other again, slower now. What could Lady Arabella possibly be doing here? How had she found out? Roseamund had taken great care to make sure this affair was as secret as possible. She knew the marriage was a farce, that Lady Arabella had been forced into the relationship. However, she also knew that Lady Arabella never tried to put a stop to the endless mistreatment of their servants; she only worked to calm Lord Tyrant enough so he wouldn't beat her, too.

Or so she thought.

Roseamund picked up her pace a bit as she neared the wooded area. Lady Arabella was partially hiding behind a tree and still motioning for her. Roseamund arrived in front of Lady Arabella and curtsied.

"Please, please don't. I don't deserve it." Lady Arabella stared down, clearly ashamed. She clutched her hands together.

"M'lady, you are the woman of the house. I would be punished for not curtsying." Roseamund's tone held both confusion and a little anger within it.

Lady Arabella looked up and straight into Roseamund's eyes. Even in the darkness, Roseamund could see that the Lady's eyes were puffy from crying.

"I understand why you would be angry with me. I am angry with myself for letting these things go on for far too long. Please understand, I live in fear myself, but I have used that fear as an excuse not to protect those whom I should be shielding the most."

Roseamund stared at her. Was this her way? Was this how she'd be able to get the children out?

Since the day Marie was murdered, Roseamund had been planning. Planning how she would slowly and quietly smuggle the children of the manor out of the lands into safety. She eventually wanted the mothers to go, too, but many of them were prominent choices of Lord Tyrant for his vices, so that would be harder. Roseamund came out of her thoughts and realized that Lady Arabella had stopped speaking and was staring expectantly at her.

"I'm sorry, mum, what was it you said last?"

"I said, I want to help. Anyway I can. I want to—"

Roseamund interrupted. This was her chance, and regardless of the fear inside her, she had to take it.

"My plan is to sneak the children out a few at a time. The stable boy has already started digging an underground tunnel from the stable to the road. If we can get enough manpower to help him, it could be done within a fortnight. Once the tunnel is stable, we can start siphoning off little ones two or three at a time and guiding them through the tunnel to the road. From there, someone will need to meet them and agree to take them to a safe house. I want to send the mothers, too, but I do not know how to accomplish that without catching the eye of the Lord."

Roseamund paused, shocked that it had all just spilled out. She had not planned to tell anyone but those who needed to know. Now she had told the female head of the household and wife of the man they were trying to evade. Roseamund didn't know if she could trust the woman, but something inside had urged her to share the plot.

"I know someone who can help. He is another Lord of a manor house a few miglio from here."

Roseamund tensed. Lady Arabella sensed the mistrust and quickly continued.

"He is my love! He is the man that I love. Lord Alberto di Turo. He is gentle and kind, believes that women are more than just objects to play with. He loves children. He has three of his own. His wife died giving birth to their third child, Angelica. He has wanted a reason to rid this land of Lord Tyrant for many years."

Roseamund smiled slightly. "I did not know you called him Lord Tyrant, as well."

A flash of anger passed over Lady Arabella's face.

"No man who treats women and children as he does deserves to be called by his God-given name. Tyrant is befitting for such a monster. His 'lord' title will hopefully be stripped of him in the future." The bitterness in Lady Arabella's voice was poignant.

Roseamund recognized the same terror in Lady Arabella's eyes she'd seen in so many others'.

"He has not left you untouched." It was not a question. It was clear that Lady Arabella had suffered the same fate as Roseamund. Likely more frequently, as it was expected of the Lady of the house to be submissive to the Lord at all times.

Tears welled in Arabella's eyes, and she angrily blinked them away. "That beast has taken more from me than I will ever be able to recover. But Lord Turo has helped me begin to heal. I steal away as much as I can." She blushed and giggled a bit. "The stable is actually the place we meet most frequently. I always give the stable boy extra rations to leave us alone for as long as he can. Lord Tyrant normally does not like to frequent the stables as he is disgusted by the smell."

Roseamund breathed in sharply. The memory of a pitchfork protruding from Marie's belly, surrounded by bloody hay, jumped into her mind.

"Roseamund, are you unwell?" Lady Arabella had stepped closer to her, reached for her arm in concern.

Roseamund came to from the flashback and quietly said, "The stable is where he raped and murdered Marie."

It was Lady Arabella's turn to breathe sharply. The color drained from her cheeks. She whispered, "All this time, I thought we were safe." She leaned forward, as if she were going to be sick. "He could have caught us at any moment! He could have killed us both!"

Roseamund reached for the Lady, helping her regain her balance. "But he did not catch you. You are still safe."

Lady Arabella caught her breath for a moment, leaned against the pine tree next to her, nodded, and then said, "For now. It won't be long before he catches on. He has spies everywhere." She turned and directly faced Roseamund. She leaned even closer to Roseamund, her voice now just above a whisper.

"Roseamund, do you have people here you can trust? Who would be willing to help?"

An excitement slowly built inside Roseamund. She *could* trust this woman. Together they were going to save these people.

"Si. Many. We've been waiting for something like this, a moment where we could finally fight back, m'lady."

A fierce gleam was now in Lady Arabella's eyes. "Good, then let us begin." She glanced around the forest, checking to make sure they were truly alone still. The night was dark and silent as death. Lady Arabella continued, "I am seeing Lord Turo tomorrow night after the Tyrant has gone to his bedchambers."

Roseamund started at that. "But m'lady, what if he wakes and sees you gone?"

"Do not fret, my child! Lord Tyrant has not visited my bedchambers since our last son was stillborn. He stopped desiring me long ago, as he has many other younger prospects he can prey upon."

Roseamund winced at that. *Like Gwendolyn.* The resolve grew within her, stronger and stronger. This must be done, no matter the cost.

"Besides, Lord Tyrant drinks himself into a stupor nearly every night. He will be dead to the world at least until dawn," Lady Arabella said disgustedly. "I wish I had a strong enough nerve to have killed him in his sleep when we were still bedding together."

The Lady's hand flew to her mouth, and she looked embarrassed.

"M'Lady, that may still need to come to pass if our plan fails. But never fear, if your hand cannot smite the devil, mine certainly can." There was so much intensity behind her words, it shocked Roseamund. "I'm sorry, m'lady. I spoke out of turn. I know he is still your husband, and I should not speak ill of my master."

"Speak ill all you want, Roseamund. He does not deserve the role of husband or master." Lady Arabella kindly placed her hand on Roseamund's arm again. "Now, I will discuss our plans with Lord Turo at tomorrow's rendezvous, and I will send a message to you through my lady in waiting. She is a trusted friend. I've known her since we were both young girls. She wants to help. She, too, had a miscarriage of Lord Tyrant's illegitimate child only a few years ago." There was so much sadness in Lady Arabella's voice that Roseamund instinctively placed her own hand on top of the Lady's.

Roseamund spoke with intention: "He has harmed us all. Now we will rob him of his vices. We will save his illegitimate children and the women who bore them, and give them the freedom to live in homes filled with love. No longer will the women and children he has tormented for years feel the pain of having to live with their abuser. We will cut him at the knees and walk away as his blackened heart decays in solitude."

Roseamund did not realize how hard she was gripping Lady Arabella's hand until the Lady gently lifted it from underneath her grasp and cupped Roseamund's face.

"Yes. We will."

Chapter Nineteen

Katie

"You're slowly walking up the staircase in five . . . four . . . three . . . two . . . one. Now you are back in the room with me. Feel the sensations in your toes and hands. Wake your body." Dr. Janet's voice floated through Katie's mind as she slowly came to and opened her eyes.

"How are you?" Dr. Janet was sitting in the chair across from Katie, her hands clasped together on her knees, the notepad she'd been taking notes on placed on the table next to her.

Katie spent a moment taking in her surroundings. The large peace plant next to the window, with its single white blossom, a halo of sunlight enveloping it; Dr. Janet's desk in the corner, neatly organized with just a few personal touches of photos of her travels; the cozy dark purple couch she was currently lying on, covered with a fluffy white blanket. It was all so surreal. Two seconds ago, she was living in her past lives, remembering so many vivid moments in each one, and now, she was here, in her current life. Was it all just a dream? Somewhere deep inside of her, she *knew* it was not. She had been all of those amazing, strong, and resilient women. She knew those traits were passed along to her in this life. She just needed to lean on them, trust them.

"Katie? Are you with me?" Dr. Janet was leaning forward, looking as if she might come over to Katie to check on her.

"Yes. Yes, I'm here. I was just—I just realized that there are things I need to do in this life that these other lives are trying to show me."

"Such as?" Dr. Janet picked up her pen and pad and sat poised, ready to write again.

Katie slowly sat up and faced Dr. Janet.

"Such as trusting my own strength and resilience. Trusting my gut instinct, and what my heart is telling me."

Dr. Janet was nodding as she wrote. Then she looked up at Katie again, pensive.

"And what is your heart telling you?"

Katie sat with the question for a moment. Her gaze transitioned down to her hands laying in her lap. She took a deep breath.

"That losing Joshua was the way I realized I am meant to be a mother, no matter how it happens. That I am supposed to write about things that matter, things that we, as a society, can change for the better. That I need to take some time for myself to really learn what those things are. And that I truly, truly want to help Jenice reunite with her mother, and help other children like her get reunited with their parents. Whatever it requires, however hard this path is going to be, I *know* this is what I am being called to do."

Dr. Janet smiled a little and nodded her head. "Good, Katie. It seems your Council and the lives you've experienced in the past have brought you to this point, where you can learn the lessons you need to learn in order to move forward physically and spiritually."

Katie felt a chill throughout her whole body, a sign she now knew was a way her body and spirit released energy. It happened when she knew things were true and also when she needed to release toxic energy. Her body's way of cleansing itself and giving her a nudge. "Yes, yes they have."

"If you decide to foster Jenice, what will you do when the time comes to give her back to her mother? How will you cope with the sadness and feelings of loss?"

For a moment, Katie was back in the days just after she lost Joshua. The pain, the emptiness that caused her to sit in the rocker in his nursery and just stare. The numbness, the darkness. The sadness. It had all been so overwhelming, she had just sat there for days, not moving, not eating, just sitting. She shook herself out of the memory and looked up at Dr. Janet again.

"When I lost Joshua . . ." Tears welled up in her eyes and she had to stop and breathe for a moment. She still was not quite used to saying his name out loud. "When I lost Joshua, it destroyed me. I completely lost my identity. I'd gone from being this badass woman who took on the world and all it threw at me by writing about it in my column, to being a shell of myself. I was the best writer at the newspaper and completely confident in my abilities to handle life. After I found out I was pregnant, I thought I could do it all—continue to be that badass writer and woman who could solve all the world's problems with the strike of a key and be the best mother anyone had ever known. I threw myself into learning how to be a good mom. I was ready. I was excited. Everything was going exactly as I planned."

Katie stopped. She sat in silence for a moment. Tears welled again.

Dr. Janet prompted her softly, "And then . . ."

"And then the world as I knew it stopped. No, it didn't just stop, it blew up in my face. Everything I trusted about myself went out the window when my son was born at twenty-three weeks and then died ten minutes later."

The tears began to spill down Katie's cheeks as she recalled those moments just after laboring for several hours. The doctors had told her his chances of survival were minimal, that his lungs were not developing correctly, that the miscarriage was nature's way of letting her know this pregnancy was not viable. But that wasn't supposed to happen. She'd done everything right! She'd read stories of babies surviving outside the womb before twenty-four weeks, and he was already at twenty-three weeks! She believed that *her* baby, with Chad's physical strength and her abilities to conquer the world, would defy the odds and prove to everyone that he would survive and beat the odds.

He had come out trying to breathe. He had been so tiny. For the first few moments, they thought he might just make it. At least, she and Chad thought so. He was clearly a fighter. Then the doctor who was working on him shook his head and turned back to the doctor who was working on Katie. Katie remembered yelling "No!" in the operating room, so angry at that doctor for just giving up. They brought the baby over to Katie and laid him on her chest. The doctor had said something about how letting him hear her heartbeat would comfort him. She remembered she could only nod. She and Chad looked at this tiny human, the little miracle they had created, and a hush fell over the room. Katie could only stare at him and breathe for him, willing him to breathe, too. But his little chest was struggling to rise. Suddenly she knew she had to name him before he left them. He had to know he *mattered* enough to have a name and that he was loved. "I want to name him Joshua," she had whispered it to Chad. He nodded, his face red and splotchy from the crying. Katie remembered thinking *I thought men were supposed to be the strong ones*. A great stillness overcame her as she witnessed her son take his last breath. *My angel.*

They let them lie with Joshua for a long time. But then it came time for him to be taken away. A nurse came up and gently said "It's time." Chad leaned down and kissed Katie and then kissed the baby and then he left the room. Then it was just Katie and Joshua.

She looked down at his tiny, perfect face and felt a love she knew she could never replicate. "You are loved Joshua. Mommy loves you." She kissed him on his small, round head, and then he was gone. She remembered how helpless she had felt. That she had done everything right and still it wasn't enough to protect this small being she had chosen to bring into the world.

"Katie, if this is too much for today, we can stop here." Dr. Janet's voice abruptly brought Katie out of her memory. The light was still haloing the beautiful lily in the window and spilling past the flower into the room.

Katie took a deep breath and shook her head. "No, no, it's time for me to deal with this. You asked me what I would do when the time came for me to give Jenice back to her mother?"

Dr. Janet nodded.

"Well, I know what it feels like to have your child ripped from you. In a different way, but I still know that loss. How helpless you feel. I would never deny a mother her chance to reunite with the child she bore and loves so dearly. I will champion the fight to reunite Jenice with her mother, so she can have that chance at that love and that connection again. I am going into this with my eyes open, that staying with Chad and me is only a stop on Jenice's journey back to the woman she is meant to be with. I will love her, and I will teach her to face whatever life throws at her while I have her. Then I will give her back to her mother with a smile on my face and a kindness in my heart because I know that is what is right. Maybe this will open the door for Chad and me to be able to actually adopt a child someday, I don't know. What I do know is that Jenice and I are meant to be in each other's lives right now, to help each other heal. That I am supposed to be her protector while we work to get her back to her mother."

Dr. Janet had stopped taking notes and was just listening as Katie said this. She smiled knowingly and nodded her head again. "Good, Katie. Very good work today. It's a lot, I know, but I believe you are right in your intentions. I will do whatever I can on my end to help you as you continue to go through this process."

Katie felt a warm glow come over her. *It really does take a village.* So many people were coming forward to offer their help as she shared what she was trying to do. It was amazing and humbling.

"So what is the next step?" Dr. Janet asked.

"The next step is talking to my boss at the newspaper. I have a feeling he's not going to like what I have to say at first, but I have some ideas for how to keep him happy while I take my leave of absence from the column."

Katie smiled, the plan for writing the op-ed about immigration practices and the process of reuniting misplaced children with their parents had already formed in her mind. She knew Sam would jump at the idea.

"Well, I can't wait to read about it when it comes out." Janet smiled at her. They stood and Katie headed out of the office and on to the street below. She had a lot to do, but now at least she knew what she needed to do.

Chapter Twenty

Katie

"Well, I can't say I'm surprised, Katie. I know this year has been hard for you. We're going to miss you around here, but if taking time off is what you need, I support you."

Sam was sitting back in his large, cushioned, brown office chair that would creak when he moved. It had been the one thing that had traveled with him throughout his entire newspaper career, and everyone knew he would keep it until it fell to pieces.

Katie sat opposite him, his desk between them. There were papers strewn all over the desktop, and Katie could see red slashes through about three quarters of the pages. She felt sorry for whichever writer those words belonged to, knowing full well what it felt like to receive sheets back that she'd poured her heart and soul into, only to see them cut through with a vicious stroke of a scarlet pen.

Sam was old school that way. While he would use the software the newspaper provided if a deadline was looming, he hated it and felt it took him more time to try to use it than to just have his writers drop hard copies off to him so he could quickly thrash through them. He was tough, but he was also one of the best and most respected newspaper editors in the country.

Katie knew this going into the meeting. She was one of those writers who fully respected him and wanted his approval at all times. They had developed a mutual respect for each other over the years, and even beyond that, he had become her mentor and she, his prized pupil. Breaking the news to Sam that she would be taking a leave of absence had kept her up the night before, terrified that she would be letting down one of the few people in her life whom she trusted and admired fully. So his response came as somewhat of a surprise. The Sam she knew often would suggest that, if the work couldn't be done at his newspaper, the person should go and find it somewhere else that would better suit their needs. The fact that he was in favor of this time off confirmed to her that this was definitely the right choice. Her nervousness melted away, and she breathed a sigh of relief.

"Thank you. Truly, Sam, you don't know what that means to me."

"I have an idea," Sam said with a knowing in his eyes. "You're not the only one who has had struggles that required changes in their life. And I'm not the hard-nosed guy you all think I am, all the time." He smiled kindly at her, a rare thing.

She smiled back, amazed at this gift she was being given. But the smile was brief. She knew how sought-after her position was, and that the reality was she would have to work her way back up when she returned. She opened her mouth to speak, but before she could, Sam interrupted by holding up his hand to stop her.

"Your column will be waiting for you when you return."

Katie couldn't hide the shock in her face at this response.

Sam laughed out loud, something Katie had never heard before. It was a deep, ringing sound that filled the room.

"Come on, Katie! You're my best writer by far! Do you think I'm going to let you get snatched up by some other mediocre paper out there? Not a chance!"

He shook his head and started shuffling through the papers in front of him. Katie sat there in stunned silence for a moment, willing herself to speak before the moment passed. She wanted to broach the subject of the op-ed.

Sam paused what he was doing and glanced up at her, his normal all-business look returned to his face.

"Well, what are you still doing here? Go! Go take care of what you need to before I change my mind!"

Katie started, then stopped. Started again, then stopped.

Sam set the papers down and clasped his hands together on the desk.

"What, Katie? Spit it out."

Katie took a deep breath and started speaking,

"I want to write an op-ed."

Sam's face developed a look of interest. "About?"

"About the inadequacies of our current immigration laws and the structure surrounding asylum seekers and deportations. About what's really happening at the borders that no one is talking about."

Sam took a deep breath in and put his hand to his face, a gesture he did when he was considering the ramifications of a story.

"That's a real hot-button subject right now, Katie. What made you decide on this topic?"

Katie leaned in and started speaking quickly. "A little girl I met several weeks ago. Well, I didn't meet her until the second time I saw her. The first time she tried to steal my coffee at the café I write at."

Sam raised an eyebrow at that but kept listening.

"She's only nine years old and a product of what happened to her when she and her mother crossed the border to seek asylum from their violence-ravaged country. From what I've been able to learn about her, they came from El Salvador and were seeking asylum in the United States. A guide brought them to the border and then disappeared when he saw the border patrol were not allowing immigrants of any kind to cross. He told Jenice and her mother a spot where they could likely cross without being seen and they attempted to cross. They were picked up shortly after and separated immediately. Jenice's mother told her to run, and at her first opportunity, Jenice did. She'd been living on the streets since then, just trying to survive, when I met her. Now she is in a group home until they can find a foster family while they find out where her mother is."

Sam was fully engaged in what Katie was saying now. "I've heard of these groups coming in and scooping up the children that are separated from their parents at the border. They fast track adoptions into American families because they feel they are 'saving' the children by keeping them from going back with their parents only for the parents to make continuous attempts at crossing the border again to find their children. There's a lot of gray area around whether what they are doing is legal. If you ask me, these parents crossing the border are trying to make a better life for their kids by migrating away from the violence and they deserve to be together, not taken in by some strange family that wants to impose their own agenda upon the kid. Do you know if any groups like this have looked at this girl? If so, that could be quite the story if what they are doing is under the radar."

"I don't know if she has been sought by those groups, but I will definitely research what they're doing. That's a good place to start." Katie had pulled out her phone and was typing Sam's suggestion into her notes. She had not heard of these groups, but she was certainly going to find out who they were and what exactly they were doing. She paused for a moment, wondering if she should tell Sam what she was planning to do with Jenice.

He picked up on her hesitation right away. He leaned back and his chair squeaked again. "Katie? What aren't you telling me?"

She took a deep breath. She knew some people she had shared this with were not sure she was ready to take care of a child so soon after the loss of Joshua, but it was what she was planning to do, and her boss needed to know.

"I am planning to foster her. And I want to make sure she is reunited with her mother as soon as possible. I don't know enough about the system to know if that's even possible. If what you say about these groups is true, they may not even be allowing children to reunite with parents who are to be deported, but I'm going to research and figure it out. That's why I think doing an op-ed would be good, because it would give me access to more than I'd be able to get to if I was just a future foster parent asking around for information. I also know there are things that need to be addressed and changed about this system, and I'm hoping maybe this op-ed could be a catalyst to help spark those conversations and hopefully lead to positive action."

Sam leaned his elbows on his desk again. He was very interested now. "Take me back to the day she was separated from her mother. Why didn't they grant asylum?"

"We don't know. Jenice said they didn't even listen when her mother was screaming 'Asylum! Asylum!' She said they just kept telling her mother to stop resisting, that things would go easier if she stopped resisting."

The frustration and anger bubbled up inside Katie. She knew shady things were happening at the border—everyone who lived in Phoenix knew it—but nothing was being done to stop it, even with the presence of occasional groups of protestors. That children were being ripped from their mothers' arms merely because they were seeking a safe place to come to, to escape the violence and death that drove them from their home, was just wrong. It was something that needed to be stopped.

"It sounds like there is a lot here to unravel, Katie. I think you should pursue it." Katie beamed and started to stand up. Sam stopped and put his hand up again, halting her exhilaration briefly. "One stipulation." Katie sat back down. "You've got to sort things out for yourself while you're doing this, Katie. Don't just use it as a distraction to avoid the things in your life that need to be fixed. Believe me, I know how that goes. I did it for years. Still do sometimes. It's what led me to be chained to this desk for twenty-five years with two divorces to show for it." His gaze softened a bit. "I need my best writer back here. So take care of yourself, okay?"

Katie breathed again and smile, determined. "I know. I will, Sam, thanks. Too much has happened now for me to ignore it. I promise you, things are getting better."

Sam nodded gruffly and turned back to shuffling the papers on his desk. "Alright then, get out of here. I expect a weekly check in on that op-ed."

The brief interlude of personal feelings had passed, Sam was back to all business. Katie gathered her bag and coat and stood. She stuck her hand out to Sam to shake.

"It's been an honor, sir. I won't let you down." She waited as he stopped his shuffling yet again and looked at her hand then up at her.

"Now don't go getting all 'sir' this and 'sir' that with me. The name's Sam, and you know it. Just go take care of yourself and get back here as soon as possible." Regardless of the statement, he did stand and take her hand, not in a formal shake, but a compassionate and caring greeting.

"Thanks, Sam. I'll see you soon."

Sam sat back down as Katie smiled, turned, and walked out of the office. She breathed a huge sigh of relief as she walked through the huge room full of cubicles and newspaper employees hard at work. A few of them glanced up at her and waved as she walked by. She smiled back at each of them kindly, knowing she'd see them again.

Now comes the hard part, she thought as she pushed her way through the double doors and out onto the sunny sidewalk and began to head down the street to her car.

Now comes the part where I try to change the world.

Chapter Twenty-One

Jenice

The two girls, Jenice and Bianca, sat in the common room. Bianca had been coloring furiously for a while. Jenice held a turquoise crayon in her hand, but it was motionless as she stared out the bleak window thinking about her mother. Where was she? Was she sad? Did she miss Jenice as much as Jenice missed her? When could she see her again? All she wanted to do was feel her mother's warm arms wrapped around her in a strong and comforting embrace, like she always did when Jenice was sad or scared. Bianca thrust the picture she was drawing in front of Jenice.

"Happy Birthday!"

Jenice, shocked out of her thoughts, looked down at the paper. It was a picture of the two of them standing around a giant birthday cake. The cake was white with colored sprinkles that Bianca had meticulously drawn in one at a time, each a different color. No two colors were next to each other, and she had included what Jenice thought was probably the entire box of crayon colors, even the brown! The candles were purple and lit up like they were ready to be blown out. The bright and cheerful picture reminded Jenice that she had told her friend she would be turning ten soon. She forgot that soon was today. A twinge of sadness and longing sped through her as she remembered how her momma would bake her a cake every year, sometimes having to make it out of whatever ingredients were in their cupboard when things in El Salvador were scarce or it was too dangerous to go out. One year, she'd made a cake out of thin, packaged sandwich meat slices and lettuce! It was the worst-tasting cake ever, but they had laughed as they ate it and Jenice only remembered how much love she felt on that day.

"It's the cake you said you always wanted, right? I tried to put as many sprinkles as I could cause I know you said you like a lot of sprinkles." Bianca was starting to look concerned that her friend might not like what she put in front of her. "I know it's not a real cake, but someday when we get out of here, I know you'll get to have a real one."

Jenice threw her arms around her friend. "Thank you! It's the best birthday cake I've ever gotten. I love it."

Bianca hugged her back and smiled. Then the two pulled apart as Bianca said, "Well, make a wish and blow out the candles!"

Jenice gigged and closed her eyes. She only had one wish: to be reunited with her momma. It was all she ever thought about; she felt it in every fiber of her body. She held her eyes closed tight as she wished the vision into existence. When she opened them, Bianca was looking over her shoulder out the door.

"Quick! Blow them out. I think we have to go to class soon."

Jenice nodded, took in a big breath, and blew the imaginary paper candles out. In her mind she could see the smoke wafting from the extinguished candles, smell the smoke. It brought a smile to her face; maybe her wish would come true. After all, birthday cake wishes are supposed to happen, right? Jenice remembered all the times her wishes had come true; she knew her momma went to great lengths to make sure they did. The biggest wish she ever worked to make happen was getting them out of El Salvador and seeking asylum. It had been a dangerous and long journey, but she had gotten them here. If Jenice had known the price they would both pay for making that wish come true, she might have wished for something else instead. But there was nothing she could do about it now. Only hope that her new wish would right the wrong that had occurred when they had been separated at the border.

Bianca was quickly throwing the crayons back in the box they came from. "Hurry and put it away! Ms. Gouch is coming!"

Ms. Gouch was a tall, domineering woman. She did not let the girls get away with anything and upheld the rules of the group home with an iron fist. Playtime and creativity were frowned upon. In her eyes, the girls were there either because they were problem children or their parents were problems and had made poor decisions that led to them being separated and having to become wards of the state. Either way, she told the children that she believed they needed to be taught that nothing comes for free in this world and only hard work and knowing right from wrong would help them become better people. To her, the children of this house were people needing to be brought into line and taught how to behave because they'd had a lack of teaching and role models in their lackluster parents.

Jenice folded up the picture into a tiny square and stuck it into her shoe. She wouldn't let Ms. Gouch take it away from her. It was the first birthday gift she had received in a few years. Last year they had been on their journey and her momma had not been able to give her a gift. "I promise you, you'll get any gift you want when we make it to America, mi amor." Her mother's gift to her the year before that had been an English dictionary. In school, they had a class to learn some English, but her momma knew they would need it when they got to the border, so she had taken her to a woman in the town who knew how to speak English quite well. She had taught them the basics: how to ask for the bathroom, how to ask for directions, how to say their name and say they only knew a little English. But Jenice had taken to learning another language like a fish to water and had begged for more lessons. By the time she got to Phoenix, she could speak it almost as well as any other nine-year-old. But knowing English had not helped her save her momma. The guards wouldn't even listen to them. The gift had not worked.

The girls stood as Ms. Gouch entered the doorway. "Girls, it's time for your class. Put those crayons back where they belong and get going before I write you up!"

Bianca grabbed the crayon box and placed it back on the bookshelf with the other art supplies. Then the girls ran past Ms. Gouch to get to their class.

"WALK! Do not run! We do not run in these halls!" Ms. Gouch shouted in her fierce tone. "If you want to learn how to fit in and be contributing members of *this* society, you must follow the rules!"

The girls sheepishly responded, "Yes, Ms. Gouch," and slowed their pace, trying not to giggle as they headed to their classroom. Today the lesson would be about proper behavior in a foster family's home.

Jenice wished they would teach more language classes, but mostly, they were about how to act right so that you didn't upset your foster or adoptive parents . . . and math and history. There was always a math and history of America class. Jenice hated math, but the history was kind of interesting. They were learning all about how America became a country during the Revolutionary War. She thought maybe, after she and her momma got settled in somewhere, she'd want to take more history classes at whatever school she ended up going to.

Right before entering their class, Bianca gave Jenice another enthusiastic hug. "I'm so glad we're friends! I hope you liked your cake. Happy birthday!"

She ran off and sat down in her assigned seat. The hug left Jenice feeling loved and remembered. *I'm so glad we're friends, too*, she thought as she took her own seat.

About five minutes into the lesson, a woman showed up at the door. Jenice recognized her. It was Aliyah, the nice lady at the café who had been with Katie. The one who had helped find Jenice a place to stay while she waited for a foster family and to be reunited with her momma. Jenice smiled and waved at Aliyah. Aliyah smiled and gave a small wave back. The teacher stopped speaking and went over to Aliyah, inquiring about what she needed. Aliyah motioned toward Jenice and the teacher nodded and turned back to the class.

"Jenice, will you come here please?" The other girls started to talk among themselves. "Girls! Silence please. No talking while I escort these ladies to the common room. Ariana, you are in charge until I get back. If anyone makes a sound, I want to know about it. Please turn to page seven in your books and begin to read." Some of the girls gave an eyeroll at the mention of Ariana being in charge, but they didn't say anything, and everyone opened their books and began to read.

Jenice got up and walked toward the door, but she turned around to look at Bianca, who glanced up and gave her a smile and a thumbs-up under her desk. She smiled and turned back around to Aliyah and the teacher.

"Follow me please," said the teacher.

The trio made their way back down the hallway to the common room that Jenice had just been in with Bianca. The teacher motioned them inside and said, "You can chat here. When you are done, Ms. Jones, please bring Jenice back to class and you can head out the way you came in."

"Thank you." Aliyah nodded as she said this. The teacher left the room. Aliyah pointed to a chair for Jenice to sit in.

"How are you, Jenice?" Aliyah asked. Jenice sat silent for a moment, studying Aliyah with curiosity. She seemed genuinely concerned for her well-being—a nice lady, like her momma.

"I'm okay. Have you seen my momma?"

"I have not, sweetheart. But I have heard about where she is." Aliyah paused, unsure of what to say next. Then she smiled.

"I have something for you from Katie!"

Jenice grew excited for a moment. Katie had been so nice both times she'd seen her. She'd felt a connection with her that she had not felt with anyone else since crossing the border. She reminded her most of her momma. Kind, gentle, but with a fire inside.

"What is it?"

Aliyah reached into her big brown bag sitting by her feet and pulled out a medium-sized, beautifully wrapped present. It was oddly shaped, but the paper was purple and the bow was silver and so pretty. Jenice immediately noticed the wrapping paper had cakes with candles on it.

Aliyah handed the gift to Jenice, who accepted it and began to examine its exterior, admiring the festive paper and ribbon. It had been a long time since she'd gotten an actual wrapped present. The past few years, in El Salvador, her mom had not been able to get her hands on pretty wrappings and would wrap her gift in magazine or newspaper. It didn't matter; Jenice always loved whatever it was her momma gave her. One year it was a doll she'd been admiring for months. Another year, the year Jenice learned how to write, her momma had gifted her a journal with a unicorn on it and a sparkly pen. Jenice felt the package in her hands. She lightly squeezed it, making sure not to tear the shiny paper, and it felt soft.

"Katie wanted to make sure you were not alone on your birthday and that you got at least one thing you could keep while you're here. I've already gotten permission from the front office. You can keep this at your bed." Aliyah nodded toward the package. Jenice's curiosity overtook her, but she didn't know if she needed to wait to be invited to open it. She looked to Aliyah for the answer, the question wide in her eyes.

Aliyah laughed. "Well go ahead, Jenice, you can open it!"

Jenice took care to untie the flowing, silver ribbon and handed it back to Aliyah, admiring its sparkles. She located the tape on the package and carefully unstuck it, trying not to rip any of the paper. As the paper fell open, an adorable, stuffed lion's face stared back at her. He was holding a big purple heart, and it had a word she did not recognize, stitched in silver, on the heart. The lion's mane was golden, soft, and sticking out from the lion's head like it had been struck by lightning. His body was plush and a lighter golden color. She immediately smiled and hugged it.

"Thank you!" she said enthusiastically. "Please thank Katie, too."

Jenice inspected every part of the toy. She looked at the word on the heart, trying to sound it out.

"Courage." Jenice looked up at Aliyah quizzically as the woman continued, "The word says courage."

Jenice looked back at the heart, the letters making sense to her now. "Courage," she repeated after Aliyah. She hugged the lion again and looked at Aliyah. "What does that mean?"

Aliyah took a deep breath. "It means you must be brave. To have courage means to have hope and be brave even when things seem scary."

Jenice closed her eyes and nodded as she kept hugging the lion. "Courage. I know how to do that."

"Jenice . . ." Aliyah quietly said. Jenice opened her eyes and looked up at the woman expectantly. "I have some news to share with you, and it is going to be hard to hear. You will need to use some of that courage now, okay?"

Suddenly, all thoughts of playtime with the stuffed lion later dropped out of Jenice's mind. She heard the change in Aliyah's tone and the words she said, and she stiffened, but she did not let go of her grip on her gift.

"Sweetheart, it's about your momma."

Jenice braced herself and hugged the lion harder.

"She has been deported."

The room started to feel cold and small to Jenice, like the walls were closing in on her. She began to breathe fast, like she couldn't get enough air.

"Back to El Salvador?"

Aliyah nodded and came closer to Jenice, putting her hand over Jenice's hand.

"But it's not safe there!" Hot tears sprang to Jenice's eyes and began to fall down her cheeks. She jumped up, away from Aliyah, and backed into the corner of the room next to the window. "It's not safe! There are bad men there! They hurt momma! They hurt me! They said they would kill us because Papa had done something against them! They took my papa! They're going to take my momma! They're going to kill her!"

Jenice was breathing so fast and heavy now that she was becoming lightheaded. She couldn't see through her tears. She didn't realize she was screaming the words.

Aliyah was kneeling in front of her in an instant. Jenice could hear her soft voice saying gentle words, but she couldn't make them out at first. Aliyah placed both of her hands on Jenice's shoulders and started to breathe in and out slowly, motioning for Jenice to do the same. Jenice closed her eyes for a moment, trying to breathe. She started to make out the words Aliyah was saying.

"Just breathe, Jenice. In. Out. In. Out." Aliyah was also slowly breathing in and out as she said this. "Jenice, open your eyes and look at me. What do you see?"

Jenice opened her eyes at the odd question, hiccupping, trying to suck in air.

"Describe what you see on my face, Jenice."

Jenice took a breath and stuttered out some words. "Nose, eyes . . ."

"What color are my eyes, Jenice?" Aliyah leaned in a bit and widened her eyes so Jenice could get a better look. Jenice focused in on Aliyah's eyes and tried to see the colors. "Brown, with flecks of gold." Jenice hiccupped again, snot and tears running down her lip.

"Good, sweetie. Tell me more. Look around the room. What else do you see?"

Jenice took a moment to really look at the room.

"A couch. Chairs. A bookshelf. Books. Some puzzles." She turned to look next to her and saw sunshine outside. She took a deep breath, "A window."

"That's it. Keep breathing. Take another deep breath." Aliyah took one and Jenice followed suit. "Good."

Jenice felt calmer. She noticed Aliyah breathing a sigh of relief. Aliyah led Jenice back over to the chair and sat her down. She pulled an ottoman close to Jenice and sat directly in front of her. Jenice held on to the lion tightly, ready to hear what Aliyah needed to say.

"Your momma has been sent back to your home country, yes. However, she is in protective custody right now. We are working hard to make sure she is safe. I have many friends and connections down there because I worked down there for several years. Did you know that?"

Jenice shook her head.

"I was just out of grad school and wanted to help people in a place that really needed it. My boyfriend at the time was Salvadoran, and he encouraged me to move there with him. I worked for one of the hospitals and saw so many people who needed care."

Jenice loosened her grip a little on the stuffed animal. "Why did you leave?"

Aliyah dropped her head for a moment. "My boyfriend and I broke up and he planned to stay. I needed to go out on my own and all of my family lived here. So I moved back home."

Aliyah reached for Jenice's hands again and looked directly into her eyes. "Jenice, I know how dangerous it is down there, and that there are a lot of bad people there. But there are good people, too, and they are going to help your momma and keep her safe."

Jenice's tears had begun to dry. She looked back at Aliyah. "Can I go be with her?"

Aliyah went to speak, then hesitated. Her eyes softened as she told Jenice. "No, sweetheart, you cannot. For you, it's still too dangerous. Your momma explicitly asked that you not be returned to the country if it was possible."

"She doesn't want me there?" Jenice felt shocked and hurt.

"It's not like that, Jenice. Your mother wants to be with you more than anything, but that is just not possible right now. We are all working very hard to figure out a way to reunite you when the time is right, but for right now, she wants you to stay here because it's just safer and better for you."

Jenice was obstinate. "But I don't want to stay here! I hate it here! No one cares! The teachers are mean! I only have one friend and everyone else is mean!" Tears began to fall again.

Aliyah nodded to the lion. "Remember what that word means?"

Jenice hugged him closer, screwed up her face in a hard stare, and nodded.

"I need to you to have all the courage you can muster right now, okay?"

Jenice closed her eyes, thinking about it, and slightly nodded again.

"Your momma and Katie have been talking." At this, Jenice's eyes flew open, and she looked at Aliyah, hopeful. "Katie and her fiancé, Chad, want to have you come live with them for right now. Your momma thinks that would be a really good idea while we try to sort all of this out."

For the first time in a long time, relief flooded into Jenice. She released her vice grip on the lion and held his hand as she dropped him to her side. She came closer to Aliyah and stood in front of her.

"I don't have to stay here anymore?" she said hopefully.

"No honey, you do not have to stay in this group home anymore. It's why I came here for you today. Katie and Chad are waiting in the front office. They didn't want to overwhelm you. They want the choice to be yours. You don't have to go with them, you can choose another foster family, but they really want you to stay with them."

"Yes! Yes! I want to stay with Katie!" Jenice jumped into Aliyah's arms and hugged her tight. Then she pulled back a bit, concern in her face.

"Can I talk to Momma?"

Aliyah smiled. "She's already written you a letter. Katie has it in your new bag. You can write to her whenever you want. She said she will try to call as much as she can, but writing is safer for her than calling right now."

Jenice smiled. A heavy weight seemed to lift off the little girl's shoulders as she took in the news. Aliyah stood and held out her hand to Jenice.

"Are you ready to go meet your foster parents?" Jenice took Aliyah's hand, carrying the lion in her other hand, and they headed out the door.

Chapter Twenty-Two

Katie

"It's taking a long time." Katie was pacing around the small, drab waiting room she and Chad had been placed in, wringing her hands. Chad was sitting in one of two chairs sitting against the wall. The door was shut, and there was a thin strip of glass next to the door where they could see into the main office.

"Katie, come sit down. Your pacing isn't going to make this go any faster." Chad reached out his hand to her and paused her nervous walk. Gently he said, "She's going to say yes."

Katie gave him a look, not as sure as he, but she sat down anyway. Her legs began to shake, a nervous tick she'd had since she was a child, that would happen when she was anxious. Chad placed his hand gently on her knee. "Breathe sweetie. It's going to be okay."

"But what if it isn't? What if she says no, or freaks out at the news of her mom and tries to run again? What if she does come with us and then she hates living with us? What if I'm not really meant to be a mother and I'm just going to hurt her further?"

The truth hung in the air like a giant pink elephant.

"Do you really believe you're not fit to be a mother, Katie?" Chad said quietly.

Katie sat for a moment in the words that had just escaped her mouth. She'd thought it so many times before. What if the reason Joshua had died was because she wasn't supposed to be a mother, even though it's something she'd wanted for so long? What if she was too selfish, or unfit, and would only destroy the life of any child that came into hers?

Katie looked at Chad, pleading for these thoughts to not be true. He grabbed her hands and turned her toward him.

"Katie, you are the most genuine, caring, selfless, intelligent, nurturing person I know. Everything you do, you do for others. Sometimes I think you should take care of yourself better because of that, but it doesn't mean that you will be a bad mother! I think you are going to be an amazing mother. I know you are scared, that you want everything to go right, but the fact is, things are going to go wrong every now and then. We know that already! Sometimes they will go really wrong. We've already been through what I think is the most wrong thing that could happen, so I'm pretty sure that whatever is thrown our way now, we can handle. You are more than capable of taking care of this child. All she needs is love and protection, to know that she matters and isn't going to slip through the cracks, and we can give that to her in spades. Her mother is entrusting her to us for a reason. I don't think she would make that decision lightly."

Katie took in the words. He was right. She knew he was right. She pulled him into a fierce hug. "I know you're right, Chad. I'm just scared."

"So am I! I don't know that I've ever met a parent-to-be who wasn't. I seem to recall Aliyah saying she was scared shitless when she was pregnant with Cassie. But look at what an amazing mother she is, and how they met the challenge and continue to meet it every day. Being a parent is the coolest and scariest thing we can do as humans! And now we get a second chance to do that." It was Chad's turn to have tears in his eyes. Katie's heart melted at the reaction. What a good man she had. His sentiment calmed her nerves.

"You're right. This is our second chance. We can help her." As she said those words, Katie glimpsed a view of Aliyah coming into the front office through the sliver of glass in their room. For a moment she appeared to be alone, and Katie's breath caught in her throat. Then a little girl hugging a stuffed lion walked in after her. Katie audibly cried out, "She's here!"

They both stood and waited as the door to the little room opened and Aliyah walked in. She was smiling broadly, and she nodded an affirmation to Katie. *She said yes.* Aliyah didn't have to say the words for Katie to understand.

Jenice stood in the doorway, a little unsure. Aliyah turned back to her gently.

"It's okay, Jenice. You remember Katie?" Aliyah motioned to Katie, and Jenice nodded vigorously. Then she glanced quickly at Chad and dropped her eyes down.

"And this is Chad, Jenice. He's Katie's fiancé," Aliyah said.

Jenice slowly looked up to Aliyah. "What's fiancé?"

They all laughed, the ice having been broken by the child's question.

Chad knelt to Jenice's level and answered, "Jenice, that means that I love Katie so much that I want to spend our whole lives together and she and I are going to get married."

Jenice looked up at Chad wide-eyed, a little nervous. "Like my papa and momma did?"

Chad smiled sadly, knowing Jenice's father had been killed long ago, and nodded. "Yes, just like they did."

Jenice seemed to warm to him a bit after this exchange. She looked to Katie, who was still standing by the chair she'd jumped out of, about to burst with happiness and concern for the child.

"And you are okay with me living with you?" Jenice said quietly.

Katie walked over, dropped to the ground, and pulled Jenice into a tight hug, love and care emanating from her every pore. Katie felt the child relax in her embrace and it warmed her heart.

"Of course! Yes, Jenice, yes, we want you to come live with us! Your momma and I are so excited for you to have a place to stay. I just want to make sure it's what you want."

Katie pulled Jenice back from her, looking straight into her eyes as she said this last part, searching for any sign of hesitancy.

Jenice smiled and nodded. "Yes, I want to. I miss my momma, but I know I can't be with her right now. You are so nice, and I like you. I want to stay with you and Chad."

All three of them breathed a sigh of relief, and when Katie hugged Jenice again, this time Jenice hugged back. Chad put his hands on both of their backs, letting them have the space, but making sure they knew he was there for them. Aliyah stood in the doorway, taking in the scene, and took another deep breath.

After a few moments, the two who were kneeling stood, and all four of them walked out of the office.

Aliyah was talking as they stepped into the brightly lit hallway. "Jenice, do you have any belongings we need to collect? Katie and I thought it would be fun for all of us to go shopping for some clothes and whatever else you might need after this."

Jenice's eyes lit up. "Shopping? At one of those stores with all the big windows with beautiful things in them?"

Katie answered, "Yes! We can go to any of those stores you want. Your momma said she wanted us to get you a pretty dress to wear to school if we could. And of course some jeans and T-shirts, too." She laughed at Jenice's face when she mentioned the pretty dress. "She also told me you might make a face like that when I mentioned a pretty dress."

Jenice giggled and Katie did, too. "I've never had one. They don't look very comfortable. And you can't climb in them." Jenice stopped for a second and looked dreamy. "But Momma always wears them, and they are so pretty."

The child's logic made sense.

"Well, maybe we can find a pretty dress that also has shorts underneath so you can climb in it." Katie's suggestion was met with a bright smile.

Aliyah interjected, "I hate to interrupt, but it looks like we need to fill out some paperwork and get going." She nodded her head toward the menacing-looking head mistress, Ms. Gouch, standing in the office doorway, tapping her foot and glancing at her watch.

"Ah yes, I see." Katie tried to stifle a laugh at the sight of the clearly wired-too-tight woman. She offered her hand to Jenice. "Are you ready? We just need to sign some things, and we can be out of here."

Jenice went to grab her hand then realized something. She pulled the lion up, looked at it longingly as if she were making a terribly difficult decision, sighed a little, hugged it, then looked at Katie. "I know this is my gift, but I have a friend here, Bianca, and I think she needs some courage, too. Can I give it to her?"

Katie felt a pang in her heart at the child's words, and a quick look at Chad and Aliyah told her that they felt similarly. Katie knelt in front of Jenice. "I gave this to you because I knew you needed courage. If you feel your friend needs courage, too, then yes, you give this little lion to her to help her remember she is not alone. We can get you another one if you like, too."

Jenice hugged Katie. "Thank you!" She pulled away from her and began to run down the hall toward the classroom that her friend was just leaving.

"No running in the hallways!" Ms. Gouch yelled after her.

Jenice stopped in her tracks then slowly made her way to Bianca. The adults could see her hand over the lion and explain what the word meant. They saw her friend start to cry and give her a big hug, the two little girls clinging to each other as if they had no one else. Then Jenice pulled back and said one last thing. Bianca nodded, hugged the lion, and stood watching as Jenice walked back to her new foster family.

Chapter Twenty-Three

Roseamund

Roseamund was gathering eggs from the hen house next to the stable when she was signaled by the stable boy, Antonio, with a light whistle. She looked to where he was sticking his head out of the stable door. He motioned to her with a slight jerk of his head to come into the stable. She put the two brown eggs she was holding in her hands into her basket, glanced around to make sure no one was watching, and headed into the stable.

Inside, Antonio was already moving a pile of tools and the hay underneath to reveal a boarded-up portion of the dirt floor. He began to lift the boards one by one and place them in the pile of hay. He removed only enough for one person to enter. Roseamund saw a wooden ladder leading down to the dark tunnel below.

"Lord Turo is waiting at the other end. It leads out onto the road on his property. You will be safe there once you are on the other side. Be careful. The tunnel is long and dark, but we have made sure it is solid." Antonio handed her a small lit torch that had been hanging on a post next to him. "Take this and your basket. We don't want anyone wondering why your basket is here but you are not."

Roseamund nodded and took the torch. "Tell Cook I've gone to pick mushrooms in the farthest field. If Lord Tyrant gets wind of it, he won't bother to come looking for me. He hates to go that far without a full escort and transport . . ."

"Which takes time to put together and will give you enough time to go and come back quickly if needed." Antonio finished her thought and Roseamund nodded back in agreement. He looked nervous but also resolved and excited all at the same time. "It's finally happening."

"It is." Roseamund felt the same. "I will return as quickly as I can. I'm hoping we can begin the crossings tonight if Lord Turo is ready."

Antonio looked Roseamund in the eye. "Don't get caught."

Roseamund felt a surge of nerves in her belly, but she took a deep breath and said, "I won't."

She set down her basket next to the opening in the floor, keeping the torch in her right hand, and began to slowly descend into the tunnel. She hesitated.

"If anything does happen to me—" she looked up at Antonio, who was now leaning down to hand her the basket "—please get them out. As many as you can."

Resolutely, Antonio responded. "I will. I promise."

Roseamund grabbed the basket dangling in front of her face with her left hand. "Thank you, Antonio."

He nodded and disappeared for a moment as he reached for the first plank to cover the hole. She watched as he placed one, then two, and finally the third plank above her. With each plank placement, the light diminished more and more until, finally, she was alone in the dark, dank tunnel with only her small torchlight to guide her. It was as silent as a grave.

This would be an awful place to die.

The thought sent shivers through her and she picked up her pace. As she walked, she thought about all the women and children that would have to pass through here and she sent a small prayer of protection that they would have the courage to face this terrifying journey.

She could hear the insects crawling on the walls around her, cockroach-
es and spiders. Suddenly a spider dropped on a thin, glistening strand of
web right in front of her and she had to stifle a scream.

*It's only a spider. It's far better than the demon tyrant you are saving
the children from. Come, Roseamund, you must keep going.*

With this thought, she screwed up her morale and swiped the spider
away.

After about twenty minutes, a soft light emerged at the far end of the
tunnel in front of her.

I've made it. I'm almost there.

Just then she heard small, scratching footsteps coming up behind
her. She froze. Clearly, it was some kind of animal. She was afraid to
look, so she just stood stock still and squeezed her eyes shut as the footsteps came closer and closer. Suddenly they were upon her!

Please don't let it attack, she prayed. And just as suddenly as they
came upon her, they were already passing by her. She opened her eyes
just enough to see that it had only been a large rat, which was probably
as scared of her as she was of it.

She let out an audible laugh and then clamped her hand over her
mouth and sucked in her breath. For a brief second, there was total silence.

"Roseamund?"

She heard a male voice at the opening. A voice she did not recognize.
This must be Lord Turo.

She sighed, relieved, and began walking again. "Lord Turo?"

"Yes, yes, it is I, Lord Turo. Are you almost here?" She could see a
man descending the ladder. For another brief moment, she froze. With
his back turned as he climbed down the ladder, he looked almost the
same as Lord Tyrant. She stopped breathing.

His voice is not the same. It is not him. It cannot be him.

The man reached the bottom of the ladder and turned. Shock came
over her face as she stared at the man in front of her. His features were
so similar to that of Lord Tyrant's she had to do a double take to make
sure it was not.

"Don't be alarmed. I know I look like him, but I assure you I am not. Lord Devaro, or Lord Tyrant as I understand he is known by, is my cousin. His mother was my mother's sister."

Lady Arabella had not shared this information with Roseamund. It was a worrisome surprise. She realized she had forgotten her station and bowed to him as best she could.

"Please, don't. You are doing myself and people I care about a great service. You do not need to bow to any of us."

Roseamund looked up at him, once again surprised. He seemed to be the man that Lady Arabella said he was, but she had to be sure. She rose to her full height and looked him straight in the eye.

"How can I trust that you will not turn me over to him? You are blood, a bond thicker than anything else." Roseamund stood rooted to the ground, terrified, but her voice did not waiver. She had nowhere to turn; she had to face what was in front of her.

"Lord Devaro severed that bond years ago when he attempted to rape and kill his aunt, my mother. He then attempted to defame her good name by claiming she had seduced him. The bruises on her neck and other places said otherwise," Lord Turo responded, distain in his voice.

Off of Roseamund's look, he continued, "Yes, his monstrous acts reached as far as his own family, the women who raised him and cared for him. He was horrible to his own mother, as well, but with my mother, Satan himself could not have attempted worse deeds."

"Is she . . ." Roseamund could not bring herself to say the word.

"Dead? Yes, but not because of him. She managed to escape the attack because I came upon them and stopped it. Thankfully a servant had been witness to the entire event and was able to defend my mother and me when we were questioned. I was too young at the time to take him on fully, but I was able to scar him enough so that he didn't try it again."

"The scar on his cheek," Roseamund gasped.

"Yes, that was from me. Now that I am fully grown and able to, I am ready to fight to the death if needed. I intend to avenge my mother and all of the women and children who have been destroyed by him." Turo's hands were gripped in fists and the muscles in his arms tensed.

"Then you and I share a mutual goal," Roseamund said, determined.

"Yes, we do. Now come, we have much to discuss." Lord Turo had reached his hand out to her.

Roseamund let out the breath she did not realize she had been holding in. She felt her shoulders relax a bit. She began to walk toward him.

"This tunnel is impressive. Aside from the spider and the rat that almost made me turn and run the other way, I'd say it was easy to make it through." Roseamund blushed a bit at her own embarrassment.

Lord Turo bellowed out a laugh, "Ah those rats can be quite a nuisance! I will make sure to try and keep the tunnel clear of them. The spiders, I cannot help as much. This is their domain; we are only visitors."

Roseamund smiled at that. She handed him the basket and torch to hold as she ascended into the sunlight. It was so bright she had to blink several times before she could truly see well. Her vision cleared in time to see Lord Turo fully in the daylight. The resemblance was uncanny. If she didn't know any better, she would swear he was his twin brother, not his cousin. Slightly thinner, as Lord Tyrant's vices had caused him to look bloated much of the time, but still, it was shocking.

Lord Turo laughed again, "Yes, I know. We could be twins. But I assure you, we are *not*." He growled this last word as he handed the basket back to Roseamund. "Come, Lady Arabella is waiting for us."

They entered a thicket of trees. It was beautiful here. Whatever dreariness existed on her own master's property, this was the exact opposite: green, lush trees, wildflowers of every color, a mossy forest floor. She could tell it was well tended to and loved by those who took care of the land. Already she could feel the stress of the situation melting away from her. She only hoped this was how it would feel for the others as they came out of the tunnel.

"Lady Arabella is here? How did she get away?" Roseamund was surprised yet again.

"She had the cook put an extra spice into Giovanni's drink that causes drowsiness. He should be out for several hours. Which gives us plenty of time to work out the details of tonight's first liberation."

Roseamund smiled at the choice of the word. It was a liberation. Then her face turned to concern for Lady Arabella. "That was quite a risk she took. She may pay for it later when he wakes."

"A risk I was fully willing to take if it meant getting this started today." Lady Arabella's voice wafted through the trees. She appeared like an angel in her beautifully spun shawl and blue satin gown on a grassy spot in front of them.

Lord Turo smiled broadly and ran up to her, lifted her up and spun her in a circle. They both laughed with happiness, hers a high bell-like giggle and his, the loud, clear bellowing laugh Roseamund had heard in the tunnel. She realized she had never heard Lady Arabella laugh before. It was clear how much in love they were. *How had she not ended up with Lord Turo in the first place?* Roseamund wondered. It was only after the fact that she realized she had actually said those words out loud.

Lord Turo answered, sadness in his voice. "My cousin had more land and was the better prospect at the time. I was still just finishing my schooling and was not yet prepared to take a wife when Lady Arabella's father was seeking a husband for his daughter."

"Alberto and I fell in love the moment we met," Lady Arabella chimed in. "I knew him before I knew Lord Tyrant, but father needed the bigger dowry."

Lord Turo caressed Lady Arabella's face gently as he said, "You were *bellissima*. A shining light at that dreary dance. You were so young, vibrant, and kind to your friends. I couldn't take my eyes off you. I knew the moment I saw you that I wanted to be your love."

She gazed back at him with love and a sense of peace in her eyes that Roseamund had only hoped for in her lifetime. It was a beautiful sight, two lovers in each other's arms, protecting each other, lifting each other up with their joy and pure contentment.

The sight brought a new resolve to Roseamund. She wanted that for all the women and children who currently lived under the reign of terror at her manor house. She never wanted them to suffer again. She stepped toward the Lady and Lord.

"I don't want to interrupt, but I do believe we need to decide on our plan of action quickly. It is nearly mid-morning, and there is so much to do."

Alberto and Arabella broke out of their reverie to face Roseamund. Lady Arabella spoke first.

"You are right, Roseamund. Your devotion to this endeavor inspires me." She spoke kindly, came up to Roseamund, and took her hands. "There is much to be done. Come, let us walk together to the spot we will bring the children." Lady Arabella looped her arm through Roseamund's and began to walk with her through the thicket. Roseamund could not get over how kind this woman was, completely disregarding her station, treating her as an equal, sharing this dangerous goal with her. Roseamund realized she admired this woman almost as much as she had admired her own mother. A warmth spread through her at the notion.

Lord Turo walked ahead of them to lead the way to the rendezvous point. The sunlight spread through the trees, almost as if lighting the path. He spoke as he walked. "Once the children have been led through the tunnel, I have two men I trust who will be leading them to this area. I will be here to meet them and lead them to my manor house where several women will be waiting to tend to their needs. Over the next day or so, we will disperse the children to their temporary homes."

"And where will those be? Who will be looking after them while we try to get the mothers out?" Roseamund's concern was palpable.

Lady Arabella replied gently, "I have many friends, Ladies of other manor houses, as well as women who live within Alberto's home, who are excited to take in the children while we work to reunite them with their mothers. Several of these women have offered to give permanent positions at their manor houses to the mothers if they wish to stay with them after this initial period. I have only asked those whom I know are happy in their households, who have not had to endure anything like we have." Arabella once again was standing close to Roseamund, treating her as an equal. But the fear and uncertainty in Roseamund's face could not be hidden.

Lord Turo picked up on her concern and added, "These men are my friends, Roseamund. I trust them with my life. All have been vetted and many stepped forward offering to help before I had even finished my proposal of the plan. They all have been affected by Lord Tyrant in some way or another. There is no love lost between them and he. They have vowed to be by my side if it comes to a battle with him."

Lord Turo's hand was gripping the rapier at his side. Lady Arabella walked to him and placed her hand on his. Roseamund could see him relax a little, the glint in his eye dulling a bit. She heard Lady Arabella gently say, "It will not come to that because we will be diligent in our secrecy while getting the children out."

"But the mothers . . ." Roseamund had still not been able to figure out how to get them out without Lord Tyrant noticing. There were so many who needed to escape.

"Will be rescued as our situation allows. I promise you, Roseamund, I will see to it that they get out." Lady Arabella's voice had developed an edge to it.

"As will I," Roseamund responded. "I am not afraid of him as I used to be. I am willing to meet my end if it means giving them a new beginning."

"Let us hope it does not come to that." Lord Turo said. "You are brave, Roseamund, braver than many of the men I know, but I will not let it come to pass that you are put in harm's way if I can stop it."

"Nor will I, Roseamund," Lady Arabella added as the two of them stood side by side, a united front. "I know how to maneuver Lord Tyrant. I know his moods and how far to push or when to pull back." Lord Turo looked with sadness and what seemed to be guilt upon his love. She had endured so much. He brushed a hair behind her ear as Lady Arabella continued. "I will do everything in my power to keep him from you so that you may do your duty."

Roseamund had never felt such love and support from two people she barely knew. Again that warm feeling spread through her. She smiled. The smile faded a moment later as she remembered the task in front of her.

"I must get back to the manor house. Cook and the other servants who are aiding me tonight must be informed of the full plan. We will begin to send the children through a few at a time starting at midnight," she said.

Lady Arabella turned to Lord Turo, and they embraced in a long, passionate kiss. Then she pulled back. "My love, I must go with her. I will return when this is all behind us."

Lord Turo embraced her again. "I will be waiting."

Lady Arabella released herself from his loving arms and walked with Roseamund back toward the tunnel entrance. He followed behind them. Roseamund could see the tears silently dripping down Lady Arabella's face. Instinctually, she reached a comforting hand toward Lady Arabella's, who gripped back tightly and squeezed once as a thank-you. The two women descended into the tunnel. Lord Turo handed down the torch and the egg basket Roseamund had originally brought with her. With one last look up at his familiar face engulfed by the majestic beauty of the land around him, the two turned and slowly made their way back through the dark, all-consuming tunnel, back to Hell.

This is it. The thought whirled through her mind as Roseamund reached the ladder at the stable. She climbed slowly and knocked three times, the signal that she had returned. Antonio lifted the boards as Roseamund climbed through the hold. She turned back and reached down to help Antonio pull Lady Arabella out of the tunnel, as well. The two women looked at each other for a moment, hands clasped together again, a reassuring squeeze coming from Arabella. Roseamund nodded and they released their hold. When Antonio had looked out the barn door and given the all-clear, Lady Arabella made her way out and in the direction of the gardens, while Roseamund headed directly to the kitchen to set the plan in motion.

This is it.

Chapter Twenty-Four

Sarah

"The woman, Sarah, she's gone."

Sarah heard the truck driver say this, but she couldn't open her eyes to tell him she was still here, somewhere. Well, maybe not here. She looked around. She could see the scene of her lying on the pavement in front of her. The truck driver, *Jim?*—she thought that's what he had said his name was—was dragging one hand through his hair and talking on the CB radio in his truck. He had tears on his face and looked terrifyingly distraught. When she looked closer at her body, she realized her eyes were open, but they were vacant looking. She realized Jim may be right. *Am I dead?*

A movement over in the trees off the side of the road caught her attention. She walked—no, it wasn't walking, more like floated—over to it. There, she experienced the surprise of her short life. A small boy stood among the forest lining the road.

"Joshy? Baby? My sweet Joshua!" Sarah rushed to grab her three-year-old son, who stood just out of her reach. He smiled at her and giggled, hiding behind a tree.

"Joshua! Please, come here, come to Momma. Why are you here?" A sudden jolt ran through her. Had Ben gotten to him? Was he dead? The thought of her son being hurt in any way, let alone dead and in this place with her, made her feel nauseous, or, not nauseous, but the idea of nauseous. She couldn't actually feel anything anymore. She was just . . . there.

"Joshy, sweetheart, please speak to me! Why are you here?"

Joshua didn't say anything. He simply giggled at her again and disappeared into the trees.

Sarah followed him, floating through the woods with ease. She tried to see where he had gone, but he had disappeared. She heard his giggle again and floated in the direction of the sound. "Joshua! Where are you?"

Sarah could sense the panic she used to feel when she could not find Joshua at home after she and Ben had fought. Sometimes it would take her an hour to find him, scared and shaking in whatever hiding hole he had managed to get himself into. It was these memories that led her to the decision she'd made.

I did it for you, baby, she thought. *I did it for both of us. It was the only way to keep us both safe. I'm sorry! I'm so, so sorry.*

She continued to follow the sound of her son's voice further into the forest.

On the road, Jim had not noticed the spectral light moving into the trees.

"Who were you, Sarah?" He looked at her ashen face for a second and then turned back to his truck, as if staring any longer at the corpse on the road was too much for him.

Chapter Twenty-Five

Sarah

The sounds of the voices around her made Sarah smile as she joined in with the solo line for choir practice. She was lucky, they all were, that the school even had a choir with how many resources had been lost to the town since the war. She smiled thinking about how many townspeople would be at the upcoming choir concert at the end of the week. The words of the song reminded her of the struggles she and her family had endured.

Being here, doing what she loved in a warm and welcoming environment surrounded by friends, was a far cry from where she had been eight years ago when her father had found her and her siblings wandering on the frigid streets of Liverpool looking for scraps of food. He had decided shortly after that to move the family to a small fishing village named Porthgain in Pembrokeshire, Wales, for a new start. His earnings from fighting in the war had allowed for the move and given him time to find work that he truly seemed to enjoy as the local tavern's barkeep and manager. They now lived in a comfortable home close to the tavern and all the children were doing much better.

As the song ended and her choir teacher released the teenagers for the afternoon, Sarah, who was now thirteen herself, lingered in her thoughts about her family and how far they'd come. She smiled again in wonderment, as she couldn't believe how tall her brothers had grown when they had both been so scrawny eight years ago. Now both James and Leo were excellent footballers, Jane had a wonderful mind for science, and little Grace was the sweetest person anyone could encounter. Opposite of her mother, although Grace was the spitting image of Lillian. Sarah grimaced at that thought and brought herself back to the room she was in. Her choir teacher was walking toward her.

"Sarah, I swear the angels take notice when you sing." Her teacher was beaming at her, but Sarah blushed at the compliment.

"Don't be embarrassed by the compliment, m'dear, it is only the truth. I know it can be hard to accept kind words from people, but you do them a disservice if you dismiss their experience. I have a feeling a lot of folks in this town will be letting you know how your singing makes them feel after this concert. It's alright to feel humble, but make sure to honor their feelings about it, too, by saying thank you."

Sarah took in the teacher's sage advice and nodded as the teacher smiled at her one more time and said, "I'll see you at tomorrow's rehearsal," before walking away.

Sarah knew the impact her singing had on the town. That it was like a balm for the people as they continued to heal from the ravages of the war. The town still held the pain of all of it. Buildings stood broken, some completely crumbling, half of them abandoned. The fish seemed to have left the area, only a few small schools each day, not enough to keep what had once been a booming fishing center as a working trade. The town was on the verge of total collapse itself, and the people there felt it, carried the heavy burden with them every day. In town meetings that Sarah was now old enough to attend, they could not agree on where to go next, how to build their industry back up, or whether to change industries completely. They'd been a fishing village for generations; it was all they'd ever known. So facing the idea that they may no longer have that ability because of the destruction and lack of product was too much for some to bear. Everyone walked around with grim faces, the weight of the world, the war, everything on their ever-weakening, collective shoulders. But, when people gathered to hear Sarah sing, their faces lightened a bit. She knew she had that effect on others with her voice, and she only hoped that, in some little way, she was helping to ease the burden that everyone felt. That maybe, eventually, people wouldn't hurt so much and the town would thrive again. A familiar voice brought her out of her thoughts as she walked out of the rehearsal hall into the sunlight.

"Sarah, swee'heart!"

Her Da was beaming at her, walking toward her while holding Grace's hand with James walking excitedly next to them. James's goofy grin made her smile back at him. She picked up the pace and ran into her father's arms in a big hug.

"Oh it's good to see ya smile swee' girl!" She felt so safe in her father's arms, knew he would always be there to protect her. "I've go' some news I think yer gonna like."

The happy glint in her father's eyes made her wonder what the news could possibly be. Before he could respond, James interjected excitedly,

"Da's gonna let'cha sing at his work!"

Sarah's eyes grew wide. "At the tavern, Da? Is tha' alright? I thought no one under sixteen was allowed."

"Swee' girl, it's allowed when you're the daugh'er of the manager and plan to sing songs t'ah'll bring joy to the patrons. "

"How many nights do I ge'ta sing?" Sarah asked eagerly.

"Three nights a week *and* we get'ta come watch ya, sis!" James's smile was ear to ear.

Sarah looked to her father again and he nodded happily. He reached a hand to hers and she took it while he gently said, "It's time to bring your gift to more folks like you've been wantin' to, Sarah. I believe yer gonna be what heals this town. Now, let's go pick up yer sister and brother and then go have a lit'le treat to celebrate."

She smiled at her father, nodded back, and then turned her head and reached her hand to her brother. James took it without a moment's hesitation. Hand in hand, the family walked down the street, heads held high, smiles on their faces.

Chapter Twenty-Six

Sarah

Sarah had been singing at the tavern now for a year. What Thomas hoped would happen had: her voice had brought joy to those who listened. This joy spread throughout the town. It got to a point where they had to put in extra seating on the nights when his little girl, now not so little at fourteen, would sing. People began to smile again. At town halls, even during the tough conversations, everyone was courteous and began to bring ideas to the table for how to get the town back to booming. Several had the idea to create a "restaurant row" where several little restaurants featuring different cuisine from around the world would bring in more income. It worked—they drew in chefs and cooks, even local ones, who brought Asian, Spanish, Mediterranean, Irish, and even American cuisine along with the regular local English fare offered at the tavern. The restaurants would buy from local towns around them along with bringing in food from the cuisine's original countries.

Word of Sarah's voice spread throughout the country, and she began to travel for singing gigs along with still singing three nights a week at the tavern. Her father insisted she maintain her school schedule, though, which limited the number of events she could sing at, much to her chagrin. He wanted her to have a well-rounded education, so she would be able to make choices for herself with the proper knowledge. She knew that he had her best interests at heart, so she stuck to his rules and continued to get straight A's at school, while in the rest of her time, she was always looking for new songs to sing. Some composers wrote songs for her and sent them in the mail, requesting that she debut their creations at whatever event they were set for. Many times, she had to refuse because the event was just too far away or did not work with her schedule, but there were several she had debuted that became part of her regular repertoire.

While singing all over the country was a thrill for her, she still enjoyed singing at the tavern the most. She knew her voice had been a balm for the town. That she had contributed to its healing. Now when she sang there, people would mouth the words with her or hum along. This made her feel whole.

One night while singing at the tavern, she noticed a young man, likely a few years older than her, admiring her. In fact, he had not taken his eyes off her all night, so much so that she began to blush as she sang a song about two lovers running off into the night.

At the end of her last set, she was leaving the small stage when she saw him rise out of his chair quickly and come toward her.

"Good evening, miss. I couldn't help but sit here enthralled by the beauty of your voice. Please, could I have your name?"

Sarah was dazzled by his face. He was charming, handsome, and endearing. She felt her name get stuck in her throat for a moment.

"Sarah," she choked out. "It's Sarah."

"Well, Sarah, I think you have the most beautiful voice I've ever heard." His eyes were a piercing blue. She sensed the intensity of his gaze and could not pull away from it. She felt she could swim in those eyes. "Would you allow me the honor of buying you a meal? I imagine you've worked up quite an appetite."

He was *so* charming. There was no way she could resist. She glanced toward the bar where her father was serving up a beer while chatting with a customer and her fluttering heart fell. She did not believe he'd be happy with this arrangement. She looked back at the soon-to-be-grown man's face and melted a bit at his inquiring eyes.

"I'll have to ask me Da," she said quietly. "He's the manager of this tavern."

The young man looked over to the bar, a slight annoyance in his face that disappeared as he turned back to Sarah. "I'll ask for you. Wait here." He turned and was off in an instant, headed toward the bar.

"No, wait!" It was too late. He already had Thomas's attention. She could see her father frown a bit at first, but the longer the boy talked to him, the more the lines of her father's mouth settled into more of a small smile, a twinkle developing in his eye. She couldn't fathom that the boy could possibly be winning over her Da. Her father loved her with all of his heart, but when it came to boys, he had very strict rules. No dating until they were at least eighteen, and even then, it had to be supervised. He didn't want what happened to him and her mother to happen to any of his children. He wanted them to all have lived a life and have a choice of what they did before saddling themselves with a spouse and children. She knew her father was doing it out of love, but she couldn't ignore the flutter in her stomach when she looked at the boy who was now walking toward her with a smug smile on his face. It was a difficult force to reckon with.

The young man approached her again and said, "Your father is quite the character! He said it would be alright to eat together, as long as we eat at the bar where, I imagine, he wants to keep an eye on us."

Sarah's heart burst into fire and butterflies. Her Da had said yes? She couldn't believe her ears. She had to work hard to suppress an expression of glee at her good fortune and instead just smiled sweetly at the young man. As he began to lead her to the bar, she realized she didn't even know his name.

"I'm sorry, I've given you my name, but I forgot t' ask fer yours." She looked shyly at him.

He looked down at her and laughed. "And I quite forgot to give it to you! It's Benjamin. Benjamin Brittle."

Sarah's stomach did another flip-flop at the sound of his name. "Well, Benjamin Brittle, it's a pleasure t' meet ya."

"Likewise, Sarah with the voice of an angel."

They smiled at each other and sat down to order.

Chapter Twenty-Seven

Sarah

Sarah slowly opened her now swelling eyes. Her head was ringing. She could barely make out the sound of her husband's voice yelling at her. He had hit her square in the nose. It had been so hard that she'd blacked out when she hit the wall behind her and crumpled to the floor. Upon coming to, the shock of what had just happened kept her rooted to the ground. She stayed very still and closed her eyes again. She knew if she just stayed submissive, he would eventually finish his tantrum and leave. He'd been harsh before, leaving bruises where he would grab and shake her, breaking things in the room, or even one time punching his fist through the wall of their new apartment, but he had never been this violent. It terrified her.

By now, Sarah was used to Ben's rages, his thrashing, accusing words, his moments of pure anger. She had convinced herself that if she could just do better, it would help calm him down, but the next fit was always right around the corner. She'd been able to cover her bruises with clothing up to this point, but now, with a large bruise already starting to show across the bridge of her nose, she didn't know how she'd be able to hide that. She'd just have to stay home until it healed. Not that she went out much anymore anyway. After a year of courting, what was supposed to be a year-long engagement cut short by the fact that she became pregnant at age sixteen, and a whirlwind marriage, Sarah's life now consisted of being an at-home wife, singing at the engagements only her husband would book for her, and preparing to bring a child into a world she was not sure she wanted to bring it into.

She was rarely allowed to see her family anymore. Her sister Jane and brother James often tried to stop by or reach out, but Ben would either tell them she was not feeling well and could not accept visitors, or he would burn their letters before she had a chance to read them. He threatened her to the point that if someone tried to contact her while he was at work, she would just say she could not talk and hang up the telephone or she would not answer the door. Her father had called the authorities a few times, trying to get her out, but Ben was always there to assure them that Sarah's father was just an overprotective man who was having a hard time letting go of his daughter. Of course, Sarah would always back up whatever he said. She was too scared not to.

On this particular occasion, what set Ben off was the fact that Sarah had not cooked the potatoes to his liking. He enjoyed melt-in-your-mouth potatoes with lots of butter and salt. Sarah had been rushed due to her morning sickness taking up much of her time earlier in the day. She'd spent more time running to the bathroom than being able to do any housework or cooking. She'd been told that morning sickness only lasted through the first trimester, and that in her second trimester she'd feel wonderful, and into her third she'd feel uncomfortable, but not sick. Not this sick at least. She'd only been able to start the potatoes about fifteen minutes before Ben had arrived home. She knew they would be undercooked and was hoping that her boiling them on high would cook them quicker, but when she had drained the water and began to mash them with the butter, they were not the consistency he would be expecting. She tried to cover it up by adding some cream to the butter. To her, they tasted wonderful, but to him, they were only another example of how she was failing as a wife.

"If you cannot even make proper mashed potatoes, how do you expect to be a good mother?" he yelled at her as she came to. "You're a useless wife, and you're going to be useless as a mother! I will not have someone so stupid raising my son!"

Ben had been convinced he was having a son all along. In fact, he had said many times that a daughter would mean nothing to him, that it had to be a son, and if Sarah was a good woman, she would make sure it was a son. Of course his delusions had no merit; daughter or son, Sarah was going to love this baby. She already did. However, she was very worried he would not love the baby if it came out the wrong sex.

What would she do if she had a girl?

She had begun to think about that. It often consumed her thoughts. She knew that most of the time, when a parent met their newborn child, it was instant love, even for the fathers. She was hoping that it would be that way for Ben, but she couldn't be sure. So she had a plan. She would take the child to her brother if it was a girl and ask him and his kind wife to raise her as their own. It was the only way she'd be able to save her from her husband's wrath. Then she would just have to try again for a boy. Her heart broke at the thought of having to give up her little girl to appease her husband, but it would have to be that way if he didn't love their daughter.

Sarah shook her foggy head for a moment. *What am I worryin' for? It's going t' be a boy.* She didn't know how she knew; she could just feel it in her bones. The child she was carrying was a boy. She'd already thought of a name for him: Joshua Thomas Brittle. Thomas for her father, and Joshua because she thought the name was strong and would suit a good boy. She knew she'd probably have a fight from Ben about the name, that he would want the child named after him, but she was willing to face that fight if it meant her child didn't have to carry his full name. She wanted her son to have something of his own, something that wouldn't remind him of the harsh lineage he came from.

She put her hands to her swollen belly and checked to make sure he was still there, still moving. In response, his little hand swished against her own. She smiled a little. She loved that feeling, that she could actually tell what limb was reaching out to her now. It would only be a matter of time before he was out in the world, in her arms.

"What are you possibly smiling about?" bellowed Ben. "Are you just too dumb to comprehend what you've just done?" He reached down and wrenched her onto her feet. A sharp pain ran through her and she bent over. "Get back in that bloody kitchen and make me a meal worthy of a husband!"

Sarah tried to move, but the pain was so sharp she couldn't even breathe. *Not now. Please not yet, it's too early.* Suddenly her feet were soaking wet. She looked down, in shock.

"What the hell? What did you go an' pee yourself? You're disgusting!" Ben roared backing away from her.

"No," Sarah said quietly, reeling from the pain. "Me water must've broken." She looked up at Ben, pleading in her eyes. "Ben, 'e's comin', the baby is comin'."

Ben's eyes grew big. He straightened up a bit. "That can't be right. He's not due for another month. You must be wrong! My son is not going to be born a weak, premature baby! You'll have to just hold him in!"

Sarah looked incredulously. *Hold him in?* This man was truly insane. How had she ever thought him charming?

Another pain ripped through her torso, and she grabbed onto the settee in front of her. She would not cry out; she would not give Ben the satisfaction of knowing how much pain she was actually in. Through gritted teeth, she said to him, "I can't just 'old him in, ya need t' call the midwife while I get set'led in the bed."

It was Ben's turn to look incredulous. "Call the midwife? No! I will do no such thing. You'll just have to go lie down and deal with this. You will not allow my son to be born too early!" With that, he stormed out of the house.

She knew he was going to the tavern and would likely be there for many hours. She waited until she could not hear his footsteps on the cobblestone street any longer before she slowly made her way to the telephone in the kitchen. It was the one commodity she had managed to beg from Ben. She claimed she needed the telephone in case anything happened to the baby. But really, she wanted it there in case she needed to call the police sometime. She reached for the candlestick handle and rotary dialed the number of the Mission House. A midwife had been checking in on her periodically throughout her pregnancy so she knew they would come. An older woman answered, "Mission House, how may I assist you?"

"I think I'm in labor. Me water 'as broken an' I keep having sharp pains. Me name's Sarah Brittle at 421 Ash. Please, can you send a midwife?" Sarah doubled over as another wave of pain and nausea overtook her. She cried out a bit.

"Yes, ma'am. I'll send someone right over." Sarah could hear the woman shuffling through some pages. "Hannah is on-call tonight. She'll be headed over shortly. In the meantime, I want you to lie down where you can. Leave the door unlocked and Hannah will call out when she's arrived and then come in. Alright?"

Sarah was salivating from the nausea. "Yes. Alrigh'. Thank ya." She dropped the phone into its cradle and looked toward the hallway. It was only about thirty feet to the bed. She could make it. She looked toward the door where Ben had stormed out and saw that it was still unlocked. *Good. I just need to make it to the bed.* She used the settee to help her begin the perilous walk toward the hallway. As she let go of the settee and took a step, the pain became so strong that she nearly fell into the curio cabinet next to the hallway entrance. Careful to catch herself and not break any glass, she lowered herself to the ground and began to crawl.

Every movement sent shockwaves through her. Something wasn't right. She knew it. Tears were streaming down her face as she continued her slow, arduous crawl toward the bedroom. *I must get to the bed. I must save him. Don't die, Joshua, please, stay in just a little longer, baby, please?* She willed her child to stay in place as she made it through the bedroom doorway and tried to pull herself onto the bed. She screamed. The pain was too much. She fell back onto the floor and lay on her back, panting, crying, begging God to keep her child safe.

Sometime later, as Sarah drifted in and out of consciousness, trying to keep her baby from being born, she heard a woman's voice.

"Mrs. Brittle? Sarah? Are you in here? It's Hannah the midwife calling. Please call out so that I can find you!"

Sarah moaned, hoping it was loud enough for Hannah to hear. She saw a shadow darken the doorway of her bedroom.

"Mrs. Brit—oh, Sarah! Alright, sweetie, it's alright, we're here now." Hannah swiftly moved to Sarah's side and Sarah saw another figure darken the doorway. She tensed, thinking it was her husband.

"N-No! No, Ben!"

Hannah looked around to her partner, confused. "No, Sarah, Mr. Brittle does not appear to be here right now, which is probably better. This is not a place for fathers to be." She motioned to her coworker. "This is Catherine, another midwife. She has come to assist me if needed. Come, let's get you onto the bed."

Hannah was assessing Sarah.

"Sarah, you've bruising across your face. Did you hit your head during the fall?"

Sarah hesitated. Now would be the time to tell the truth. Maybe they could help her. But the threat from her husband still lingered in her mind. *If you tell anyone, I'll kill you and the baby.*

"Y-yes. Yes, on the bedside table corner."

Hannah didn't look convinced, nor did Catherine, but she nodded anyway. She tried to pick Sarah up from the floor. Sarah let out a screech and nearly pulled Hannah over on top of her.

"Alright, Sarah, it's alright." Hannah looked quickly to Catherine. "Grab her on the other side. We will need to lift her."

The other midwife hurried to Sarah's left side, and together with Hannah, they lifted Sarah onto the bed. Sarah cried out again. "Somet'ins wrong! It's too early!"

Hannah spoke calmly. "Sarah, I'm going to examine you to see what is happening with baby. I want you to lie back on the pillows there. You're going to feel discomfort and a little cold."

Sarah lay back on the white pillows that Catherine had just set up behind her. She looked at both women in their red sweater and cap with blue uniforms underneath. She had come to trust these women with her life. She knew they would do everything they could to save her child. She tried to breathe as Hannah lifted Sarah's brown skirt up to her knees.

"There's some bleeding, Sarah. We need to move quickly so that the baby can get out and breathe."

Sarah started at that. "He can't breathe? Please! Please help him!"

Catherine placed a cool cloth on Sarah's sweating forehead. "Shhhh, Sarah, we are helping him. Hannah is the best midwife in this town. Try to stay calm so she can do her work."

Sarah's mind was going a thousand miles a second. *What if the baby died? What if he died before she could even meet him? What would Ben do?* He might kill her if she lost his baby. She began to hyperventilate. She prayed that if this baby died in her womb today, that she would die with it.

"Sarah, I need to you breathe deep and slow. In. Out. Come on, in. Out." Catherine was speaking to her in a firm tone. Sarah followed the woman's breathing demonstration and calmed a bit. "That's right. Good girl."

"Catherine," Hannah said quickly. It was an order, not a request.

Catherine left Sarah's side and went down to where Hannah was between Sarah's legs.

Sarah could barely make out the words they were saying.

"The baby is breach. We will need to turn it and get it out as quick as possible. We only have minutes. She's losing too much blood. Once the baby is out, we must call the ambulance," Hannah said quietly.

She knew her baby's life hung in the balance. She also could feel that she, herself, was slipping away. She would not give up until he was out and breathing.

"Save my baby. Save him."

Hannah and Catherine both looked up to Sarah with intent in their eyes. Hannah spoke, "We will be saving you both today, my dear. Now I want you to scoot to the edge of the bed and sit up slightly. We are going to place your feet as high as they will go."

The two women helped Sarah slide down to the edge of the bed and position herself at the edge. Catherine held one of Sarah's feet and pushed her leg up in a squatting position, while Sarah tried to hold her other leg in the same position.

"When I say go, I want you to do small pushes. Then we must wait and let the baby rest a moment. I will try to turn baby, and when I say go again, you will push again." Hannah's orders were clear and decisive. "This is going to be more pain than you've ever experienced, Sarah. Get ready."

Sarah prepared to bear down. She nodded to Hannah. "I'm ready."

"Here are the baby's feet Sarah. Now, small pushes Sarah."

Sarah began to push. The pain was so intense she was seeing stars, but she kept pushing. She had to help her baby come into the world no matter how much it hurt. She continued, panting breath, wanting to just push hard, to get the little body out. It took all of her will to push slowly.

"Alright, Sarah, you need to stop pushing. Now I will let baby rest for a moment, and then you will help baby's head come out fully."

Hannah glanced up at Sarah, who was feeling panicked. "Just breathe slow, Sarah. Just for a minute." To Sarah, the minute felt like hours. She had gone numb from the pain. Finally, the minute was over.

"Now! Now, Sarah! Push!"

Sarah bore down and screamed as the baby's head finally cleared her body. The sense of relief when its head came free was like breathing again after holding one's breath underwater for too long. Sarah gave a soft groan of happiness that it was finally over.

"It's a boy, Sarah." Hannah's voice came through Sarah's reverie.

A boy. My sweet Joshua.

She listened for her baby's cry, but no sound was coming from the tiny blue infant now in Catherine's hands. All the relief and joy Sarah felt a moment earlier turned quickly to anxiety.

Catherine was rubbing the baby furiously with a blanket. She barely glanced at Hannah, but Sarah caught the look.

"Why ain't 'e cryin'?" Sarah said frantically. "Why ain't Joshua cryin'?"

Hannah looked up from where she was waiting for the afterbirth to leave Sarah's body.

"Baby just had a trauma and is in shock, Sarah. Give it a moment."

They all collectively held their own breaths as they waited for baby Joshua to take his first breath. Catherine continued to rub.

After what seemed like an eternity to Sarah, it finally happened—Joshua took his first breath, and a wail from the small child filled the room. All three women began to breathe again, and Catherine brought the baby over to Sarah, who was laughing and crying at the same time. She eagerly pulled him to her chest and, for the first time in her life, as she looked at her newborn's beautiful face, she finally knew what unconditional love meant.

"What did you say his name was?" Hannah asked, smiling gently at mother and child.

"Joshua," Sarah whispered. *My Joshua.*

Chapter Twenty-Eight

Katie

Katie gasped awake.

"Joshua!"

She was disoriented for a moment. The memory was so real, she thought she was still in 1950s England having just given birth. Her insides ached when she realized it had been a dream or flashback to another life. Her spirits immediately deflated at the realization. She looked around and her surroundings came into focus. She was sitting at her mahogany desk in her and Chad's apartment. Chester, who'd been resting comfortably in her lap until her outburst rudely interrupted his slumber, had fallen off her lap onto the floor and walked away grumbling. In front of her, the laptop lay open to a page about immigration policies for asylum seekers in the United States. Apparently she had fallen asleep while researching for her op-ed.

Joshua. She named him Joshua.

A sharp pain gripped her heart at the thought of her son. She knew she'd named him Joshua for a reason, but when the nurse had asked what made her decide on his name, she couldn't tell her. Now she knew it was a name that had been with her for a long time. She wondered if Sarah's Joshua had survived past that first breath.

Please, God, please let him have lived.

The tears came hot and fast. She had not expected this. Somewhere in her past, she'd had a son, and she'd named him the same name as the son she'd lost in this life. The connection was so strong, it took her breath away.

So much of these women's lives, her lives, took her breath away. Anya with her strength and knowledge, Roseamund with her courage and tenacity, and Sarah with her beautiful singing gift and now her son. They all possessed things that Katie wished she had, and yet they all had things she knew she had deep down inside. The parallels were uncanny. Katie knew from her sessions with Dr. Janet that often a spirit chose to live another life because they still had a lesson they needed to learn.

What lesson am I supposed to be learning in this life? Grief? Sarah, Roseamund, and Anya had all experienced that. Overcoming? Again, all of them had experienced this.

Katie glanced at the page on her computer again.

Motherhood?

Maybe this was it. Being a mother was something she wanted so badly in this life, and clearly, she had been a mother-type figure in all of her past lives. Maybe there was yet to be a lesson learned about being a mother in this life.

She turned to look at the bedroom door that was now shut because Jenice was sleeping, and Chad was sleeping in the other bedroom, because it was three in the morning. Katie had been struggling to sleep at night since Jenice came to their house, wanting to make sure she was okay, wanting to research for her op-ed without interrupting her time during the day with her. She would be starting school in a week, and Katie wanted to make sure she was comfortable and had everything she needed before then.

They had gone school clothes shopping yesterday. Katie smiled at the memory. Jenice had been so wide-eyed, touching every garment. She kept exclaiming how beautiful everything was. She told Katie the last time she'd had a new set of clothes was for her birthday two years earlier when her momma had saved up and bought her a beautiful, flowered blouse. Katie remembered Jenice's face as she described it: "deep red with little black flowers all over it. It was so soft to wear! I loved it so much." Then Jenice's face had fallen, and Katie had asked her what was wrong. "I had to leave it back home when we left for our journey. Momma said it would only get destroyed because the journey was long and difficult. She was right. By the time we were at the US border, I only had the shirt and pants I was wearing." Katie remembered having no idea what this child had been through, wanting to empathize with her but having no experience even remotely like that to compare it to. She had given Jenice a hug and offered to buy her a new flowered blouse, to celebrate being in her new "for now" home. Jenice had thought about it and then had said, "Could I have new pants and a t-shirt instead…and maybe that dress momma said I could get?" Katie had nodded, understanding that to Jenice, likely a new blouse would not be able to replace the beautiful one she'd had to leave behind in El Salvador. She had felt silly for offering to buy it and hadn't brought it up again.

How am I going to care for this child? I barely know her. I don't really know what she's been through. I don't know anything about her home or her culture. I don't want her to lose any of that because she's with us.

Katie looked back at the screen again. "Immigration policies in the United States 2020" was staring back at her. She could start here, to try and understand what was *supposed* to happen for asylum seekers, and then she would seek the stories of those to whom it was really happening. She also wanted to begin learning about the culture in El Salvador. What was everyday life like there? If Jenice was willing, she would interview her, but she didn't want to trigger or jeopardize her in any way, so she figured she would start with her mother first. They had been communicating whenever possible through letters and emails when Mariana could access it.

Katie sat up again and turned to her computer. *Anya believed the best way to know someone was to learn about their ancestry, their culture. Roseamund tried desperately to save her culture by saving the children, and Sarah . . . was running away from hers. Who came out better in the end?* Katie knew the answer was Anya, and eventually Roseamund, although she wasn't sure how for Roseamund yet. She could still only remember up to the point of the night of the first tunnel escape. But somehow a deep knowing told her she turned out okay and so did those children. That she helped them create a new life for themselves while holding on to their maternal lineage, at least.

Because I think they would want to forget their paternal lineage. Katie stopped looking at the screen for a moment, recalling what a horrible entity Lord Tyrant was.

"If I had lived through that, and he were my father, I would want to forget," she stoutly said to Chester, who was now glaring at her from across the room. He had settled himself neatly onto their couch, on the little red blanket they had set up for him so his fur wouldn't cover the couch linen. Then she changed her thought process. "Or maybe not. Maybe there is something to be said for knowing where you came from, no matter how bad it was, so you learn who and what you don't want to become."

She turned back to the computer and typed into the search bar "El Salvador violence and refugees."

"If I'm going to write an entire piece about Jenice and her story, then I have to know all of it, the good and the bad," she said to Chester, who had already put his head back down and only feigned to be listening by turning a single ear toward her.

So many articles popped up that she wasn't sure where to start.

"Okay, I guess I'll start at the top." She pulled out a large notebook where she kept notes on pieces she was writing and turned it to a blank page. "Here we go." She clicked on the first article. It was all about the violence, one statistic reading that a woman in that country was murdered every twenty hours. It talked about how violence has stemmed from decades of civil war and gang violence and likened it to being as violent and war-torn as countries like Syria.

"Oh my god." Katie had her head in her hand as she read. It was shocking. She could only imagine what Jenice and her mother had faced while trying to escape. Syria she knew about—it was always being reported on in some news precinct—but why was no one talking about what was happening in Central America?

Hundreds of thousands of displaced Salvadorans tried to flee the country each year according to one article she read. Some were taken in as refugees in Mexico, which didn't have much better of a report regarding gang violence, but many tried to make it to the US border to seek asylum. In recent years, the US had started deporting asylum seekers back to El Salvador without granting them a hearing first. Families were being torn apart as parents were separated from children at the border. Many children were being picked up by adoptive US families without ever knowing what happened to their parents. It was an absolute nightmare and horror.

Katie had known the immigration system needed revamping—living in Phoenix, one is well aware of ICE and what is rumored to happen during raids and at the border—but to read it from source after credible source, to have a child in the next room who was living it, was eye-opening for her. She began to feel a little like she felt when she was dreaming of Roseamund's life: resolved, like she needed to *do* something to help change it. This piece would be a start, but she had to do more. She didn't know what yet, but she knew it had to be more.

Katie glanced at the clock: 6:00 a.m. She'd been reading for three hours! She quietly turned off her laptop and closed it. She snuck back to her bedroom and, with one glance toward Jenice's door, she opened her own and went to get a little sleep before everyone woke up.

Chapter Twenty-Nine

Roseamund

"You must go, Gwen! It is imperative that you leave tonight. Lord Tyrant is on the warpath since he has discovered children going missing." Roseamund was adamant as she plied the large doughball on the wooden counter in front of her.

"I'm not leaving without you, Roseamund. You're the only family I have left." Tears welled in Gwendolyn's eyes as she stood rolling out dough across from Roseamund. They were preparing the evening's dinner bread. Roseamund huffed and pounded her fist into the dough in front of her.

"I know, but you are not safe here. Lady Arabella and I have had to thwart his advances on you too many times in the past few days. You must leave before he has a chance to get his meaty paws on you. I don't know what he'll do to you if he does." She continued to pound the dough, knowing full well she was over kneading it but not caring. The bread be damned. Let Lord Tyrant eat tough bread.

Tears were streaming down Gwendolyn's face now. "But how will you get yourself out?"

Roseamund stopped hitting the dough and felt compassion seep in. This poor girl had lost everyone she loved. She made her way around the counter and enveloped Gwen in a fierce hug. "I will find a way. I have survived thus far. I will keep fighting and surviving." She pulled back from Gwen. "But not until I see to it that the women in this manor house are safe from him."

At Gwendolyn's face, Roseamund softened again. "And I promise to make that as soon as possible, alright? But it will be easier to do that if I don't have to worry about you, too."

Gwen nodded solemnly, perhaps not fully trusting her response, but unable to muster a retort. The two girls got back to their kneading and rolling. Roseamund lowered her voice to a soft whisper and leaned toward Gwen.

"Now, tonight, you must be there at midnight sharp. I will help you find the way, it will just be us, as it has become too dangerous for Antonio to keep watch at such an unusual hour. We will have to be silent and vigilant about moving quickly. Once you are on the other side, we will knock three times to give the signal to open the trap door at the road, and you will be safe. Promise me you will not try to follow me back." The young girl did not respond right away and Roseamund looked sternly at her. "Gwendolyn . . ."

Finally, Gwen reluctantly nodded in agreement. "I promise."

Another servant woman walked into the room and the conversation ended. It was an unspoken rule that only the mothers, children, and cook were safe to speak around. Roseamund swiftly changed the subject—"Gwen, you need to roll a bigger circle"—and the girls got back to their work.

It was just after midnight and Gwendolyn was late.

Where is she?

Roseamund's anxiety was peaking as she hid behind the stall next to the trap door of the tunnel. Suddenly she saw a figure moving toward her. She held her breath, as she did every night she had to lead this expedition, worried that it would be someone she didn't want knowing about what she was up to. Her breath heaved out quickly as she was able to make out Gwendolyn's small frame.

"Rose?" Gwen looked nervous as she barely let out the whisper.

"Here, Gwen. Shh. We must be as silent as possible." Roseamund reached for Gwendolyn's hand and guided her to where she was standing. She motioned to Gwen to stand still and stay silent. She then went to work lifting the heavy trap door to the tunnel. It was hard not to groan at the weight, but she was able to lift it enough to create a small hole, large enough for each of them to fit through. She grabbed the unlit torch, tinder box, and fire steel that were laying hidden underneath the hay next to the opening. She motioned to Gwen to climb down. Then Roseamund followed her slowly. She stopped midway on the ladder to hand Gwen the items so that she could slide the trap door mostly shut. She had to leave a small sliver open so she could get back out when she returned. She had gotten so used to doing this over the past fortnight that it wasn't so difficult anymore. She then climbed the rest of the way down.

"Here, hand me the tinder box and fire steel, I'll light the torch once we are a ways from the opening." She felt a small box and cold steel shoved into her hands. They began to feel their way along the corridor.

"This should be alright," Roseamund spoke softly as she stopped and halted Gwendolyn too. Somewhere down the tunnel they heard scratching noises.

"Wha-what was that?" Gwendolyn shivered.

"Lord Turo had promised to clear this place of the rats, but even he cannot keep them all out. Don't worry, they are more scared of you than you are of them."

Roseamund struck the steel against the tinder box several times before a flame erupted. She led the flame toward the torch and gasped as it exploded into larger light.

"Yes, the rats can be so bothersome in places like these."

In an instant, a knife was around Gwendolyn's neck, and the Lord Tyrant's face glowed menacingly in the flickering flame of the torch that now lay on the ground next to him. In her shock, Gwendolyn had dropped it, but it had not gone out. Roseamund's stomach dropped, and she felt bile rise up in her throat.

"Let her go. You do not need her. You have me." Roseamund spoke low and slow, hoping he would hear the threat in her voice.

"Ah, Roseamund, so temperamental, so unwilling to let anyone else have any fun." Lord Tyrant's grip on Gwendolyn tightened as the knife etched a tiny line of blood into her neck. "Pick up the torch, turn around, and walk, or she will go the same path as her mother." His voice had dropped into a growl. "And if you even think of using that as a weapon, know that she will be dead before you can turn around."

Roseamund tried not to show her trembling as she picked up the source of light. She gave him one long, terrible glare before she turned and walked back in the direction they had come. She could hear his and Gwendolyn's steps begin to shuffle behind her.

"You know, you really must take more caution when gossiping in the kitchen, girls. You never know who might walk in on your conversation." He laughed as he said the words. "Poor Annabeth couldn't refuse when I made it known it was her life or yours."

Roseamund squinted her eyes shut for a moment. She knew she shouldn't have been talking so loud earlier in the kitchen. But she had trusted that everyone in there would keep their mouths shut, as the kitchen had always been the one safe haven where they could speak freely about the horrors of the house. She had not realized how close the horrible man had gotten to figuring out who was behind the children disappearing. She cursed herself under her breath for having put Annabeth in that position.

She reached the ladder and stopped. Would anyone hear them? Would he kill them right there? She knew likely not. Lord Tyrant liked to play with his food before he killed it.

She tried desperately to think of any way she could fight back without putting Gwendolyn in harm's way, but nothing came to her. She closed her eyes. A single tear fell down her cheek. *I've failed.*

"Climb, wench!" His outburst startled her into movement. She slowly made her way up the ladder, torch in hand. At the top, she precariously slid the trap door to the side, first using her finger tips with her free hand while balancing on the ladder rung, then forcing the torch hand through the opening and shoving it further open with her arm. She could feel a bruise forming immediately on her forearm, but she continued to push until there was enough open space for her to climb through. She was roughly grabbed from above, and the torch was ripped from her hands. Two of Lord Tyrant's henchmen were waiting for her in the stable.

"Gag and tie her and take her to the Cage. I'll deal with her later."

Rosamund tried to struggle, but the men were too strong for her. She screamed as a wretched-tasting cloth was shoved in her mouth and then another wrapped around her head. A rope was tied around her hands. Tears were falling freely now as she watched one of the men reach down and easily pluck up Gwendolyn, who was so scared she seemed to have gone into some sort of shock. Lord Tyrant pulled his fat, bulbous body out of the tunnel, adjusted himself, and spat at Roseamund's feet before he grabbed Gwendolyn again, threw her over his shoulder, and walked off into the night.

Roseamund's heart was racing. There was no way out for her at this point. She could only hope that Gwendolyn would be submissive so as not to invite any more violence upon her. Thinking of it made her want to vomit again. She also hoped that somehow Lady Arabella had been able to get away, to get the news to Lord Turo. He was their only chance of stopping Lord Tyrant now. He had said he would fight him if it came to that . . . and it had.

She was pushed roughly from behind.

"Walk!"

The man who pushed her was a known spy for Lord Tyrant. He was almost as horrible as the lord himself. She glared at him but began to walk.

The Cage was a horrible, dank, dark room where Lord Tyrant liked to put the servants who he felt wronged him in any way. One time a young man who had spilled some water on the table while pouring his glass had spent a week in the horrible place. He was never the same when he came out.

Roseamund prepared herself to be in there much longer than that. She could only hope beyond hope that, if it came to a battle, someone would find her there and let her out so she could fight, too. It was all she wanted at that point, to fight the man who had made so many people's lives a living hell. The thought of finally bringing him to his knees so he could have proper justice served against him consumed her as she was shoved again, this time into the hole that was the Cage. She felt hands untie the gag around her mouth.

"Now don't you go thinking you're going to yell for anyone. There ain't nobody around to hear you."

She choked out the cloth that had been in her mouth and turned around just in time to see the man who had shoved her leering at her as he closed and locked the door. Her hands remained tied.

"It's too bad Lord Master has pegged you for his own. I would've liked to have had my way with you."

She had just enough time to spit in his face.

He made a guttural sound and lunged at her, but the door thankfully kept him from being able to hit her.

"Never mind, I can see you're not worthy of what I would have given you, bitch."

He sneered and walked away angrily.

Roseamund fell back against the wall of the terrible-smelling cell. She tried desperately to pull her hands loose from the knot around her wrists, but it was no use. She slid down the wall in a heap, hot tears bombarding her yet again.

You fool. How did you think you could ever get away with this?

As she vainly tried to listen for sounds of anyone who might be able to help her, a cold chill came over her.

Please God, if there is a God, please let them get to Gwendolyn before he does too much damage.

Her sobs filled the tiny room as the first signs of early morning began to peek through the cracks of the door.

Please God. Help us.

Chapter Thirty

Anya

"Bring him over here!" Yaari shouted as another set of soldiers was seen carrying a barely conscious warrior between their shoulders. "And make sure to use the tincture before you leave."

Anya watched as Yaari motioned to a clay bowl full of clear liquid, a sanitizing concoction they used to keep their hands clean. Yaari sternly said to the soldiers, "You do not want to catch this yourselves. Please."

The two soldiers glanced at each other nervously as they set the sick man down onto a mat, one of several dozen laid out around the healing hut. They hurriedly went to the bowl and washed their hands and faces with the tincture before heading out again. As they left, one turned back to speak—it was Amaruq. Anya watched as Yaari's face registered who was in front of her. She noticed Yaari went from completely focused and intense to looking up at the soldier with joy and love in her face. Anya smiled; she knew these two were meant for each other.

Amaruq spoke gently to Yaari: "There are many more, my love. So many more."

The sadness in his voice caused Anya's her heart to lurch, and she could see the love in Yaari's face turn to resolve. Anya studied Amaruq's strong but worn-looking face. Dark worry lines had developed around his eyes and mouth over the last several weeks. So many were ill now, with no end in sight and no cure. She softened at the yearning in his eyes as he and Yaari continued to look to each other. Anya knew these two would take the marriage rites of their village. Just like she knew Yaari would one day take over for her as medicine woman and leader of this village with Amaruq by her side. They would survive this, and she would be his wife, and they would lead their village, strong in their union to each other and to the greater good of their people.

The vision brought a sense of calm to Anya as she watched Yaari stand and say to Amaruq:

"And you will keep bringing them here, and we," she motioned to Anya and then down the line of warriors, women, children, and elderly lying on the mats, "will continue to try to heal them."

Anya could see that the strength in Yaari's eyes and voice gave Amaruq new resolve. He stood straighter, took a breath, nodded, and turned to his fellow warrior. "We will continue to search all huts and the surrounding trees until all villagers are found and brought here." The soldier responded with a conceding "Yes, sir," and headed off toward the next hut. Amaruq lingered for a moment, and Anya could see him admiring his soon-to-be wife. She watched as Yaari gave him a small smile in return.

"Be careful, my love. You must stay safe and healthy so that we may save them all," she said quietly. Amaruq nodded and left, and then Yaari knelt back down to tend to the sick man in front of her. Anya knew the man was burning up with fever, almost seizing with chills, but she trusted her apprentice to use her gifts to help him. She watched a moment longer as Yaari pressed a cold cloth to the man's forehead and began to chant as she ran her hands over his body, checking for where the internal signs of illness pooled the most so she could slowly try to draw out the disease.

We must find a cure, nothing is helping yet. The frenzied thought broke Anya from standing witness to her novice, and she returned to her own patient, the resolve to help her find this cure and save their people even deeper. She focused on a spot she felt within the woman lying in front of her and closed her eyes, chanting loud, using all her skill and gifts to clear the darkness, and she felt the woman relax and start to breathe normally. Anya sat back and watched as Yaari did the same with the man next to her. Her apprentice was now becoming the master before her very eyes, and she couldn't be prouder. This child who had nearly died in her arms was now holding a dying man in her own arms, willing him to hold on long enough so that they could find a cure for the terrible disease wreaking havoc on the tribe.

"Fear not, child. Your strength is keeping these people alive. We will find the cure." Anya knew deep in her bones this was the truth as she placed a warm and calming hand on her mentee's shoulder. Yaari's shoulders visibly relaxed and Anya knew the warmth was calming her as it spread through her body. Anya was using her own talents to help Yaari stay focused for the task at hand.

"Let me take over for a while. We are running low on supplies and your eyes are better than mine now for searching."

Yaari started, about to protest.

"Please. Yaari, go. We need more dillweed and lavender. I think I saw some on the north side of the forest yesterday."

Anya noticed her gentle request coaxed Yaari out of the fearful look on her face and into a state of duty. She rose, nodded, and headed to the door. Just before she disappeared into the hole of the hallway, she turned, tears in her eyes but also a resolve Anya had never seen before, and said, "Mother Anya, we *will* defeat this." And with that, she was out of the hut.

Anya received the emotions the child had left behind in the room. "I have no doubt in my mind." She knelt next to the man to whom Yaari had been tending and began the ritual of setting his body to sleep so he could rest. In the back of her mind, Anya sent a prayer to Mother Earth that somehow she would help them save her people, yet again.

Yaari burst into the healing hut. She dropped the basket at the door and ripped an unfamiliar looking plant from the top of the basket, holding it high for all in the hut to see.

"I've found it! It's here! The cure is here, Anya! We're saved!"

Everyone in the hut stopped what they were doing. Amaruq was holding a sick child as Anya poured liquid into her mouth. Anya looked to Amaruq for a moment, seeing a flash of hope and concern in his eyes, stood calmly, and made her way around the bodies on the ground to her young apprentice, who was staring wild-eyed and flush-cheeked back at her. Anya placed her hands over Yaari's and the plant she was holding in them and asked, "You are sure?"

Yaari excitedly responded, "I came across it while I was foraging in the forest. I had never seen the plant before, but something made me stop to look at it closer. I prayed to Mother Earth and Father Sky to show me the healing properties of this new plant. I am sure. This is the cure."

Anya closed her eyes with her hands hovering over the plant, and then she opened them quickly and stepped back, a rush of emotion coming over her. She took Yaari up in an embrace only a motherlike figure could give. Then she pulled back with tears in her eyes.

"You are right, my child. This is the cure."

Chapter Thirty-One

Katie

Katie awoke with a sharp intake of air.

"They found the cure."

She turned her head to the left at the sound of her fiancé quietly snoring and smiled. She realized that he was not unlike Amaruq. He was gentle and loving, yet in times of crisis, he was a rock, the type of person she could trust to be there, going through whatever it was side by side with her while also supporting her to lead the way if needed. A warmth began to spread through her chest as she realized how lucky she was. Her thoughts drifted toward Sarah and Roseamund. How women of such strength and courage could make it through what they had was beyond her. She felt a twinge of shame as she realized she had never had to deal with the abuse those two women endured. Much like what Jenice's mother went through in El Salvador. The abuse and violence that had prompted her to leave everything she knew—her home, family, friends—and steal away with her child in the night in hopes of making it to a place that would be safe for Jenice to grow.

What we do for our children.

The thought gave Katie pause. She made her way quickly to her laptop and opened to the blank page that was her op-ed on immigration and the border crisis. She had struggled to begin, the sheer weight of the story causing her to panic and develop writer's block. Now, she knew where she had to start.

As adults, we are so busy combatting the constant barrage of society's expectations, the world's traumatic events, our own events, work, and home, we forget what it's like to just be in the moment. To just live in the innocence of what humanity can be, the way a child innately does without thinking about it. This is why we do for our children what we might not do for each other. Their innocence, their complete and utter presence in their emotions, it's something to cherish and protect. It's why we not only protect our own children, but all children. Or at least we try. What's happening at the border of this country right now is something that must be addressed. Not because of the "US or THEM" mentality, but because of the children. Thousands upon thousands of children are being abused or abandoned, not by their parents, who are coming to this country in hopes of a better life for their children, but by individuals and groups in our society who don't believe that helping an innocent child live a good life is a priority. It has become political, monetary, and about everything but the welfare of the child. It is time to bring the focus of the border crisis back to what it needs to be about—the children. It is time for us, as adults living in a collaborative and worldwide society, to take our focus off ourselves and turn it to the lives of those we've created. The saying "It takes a village" has been ignored in recent years, but that is exactly what we will need to bring the changes necessary to help these children not only survive, but thrive. And by village, I mean all of us, every single human being in this country capable of caring for others. We all are part of living this thing we call life. We all have a responsibility to help those innocents who did not ask for what they have been given or what has been taken from them.

Katie dropped her hands to her lap, where Chester the cat was now plopped and purring, and heaved a sigh of relief as she stroked his fur, her hands shaky with adrenaline. She let his purr calm her as she took a few more deep breaths; she'd been holding her breath the whole time she typed. It seemed those words had been sitting inside of her, building up, just waiting to burst forward for quite some time, like a kettle about to whistle. She reread what she had written, nodding as she went, feeling the call to action. She also knew that it was going to sound many alarms and cause a lot of debate.

"Good!"

Chester jumped at her outburst and walked away, griping with sounds only a cat can make. The sounds weren't loud, but after the silence of the room with only clicking of the keys and purring from the cat, it seemed louder than normal. Katie chuckled at the kitty as he stalked away, tail straight in the air.

"I imagine that's how a lot of people are going to react, Ches." Her smile became serious. "But these conversations need to start happening or more children will end up where Jenice was, or worse." She shuddered at the thought of any kids having to face the atrocities of what she knew was happening at the border, out of sight from the people who wanted to help. So many little girls and boys were being torn from their parents, only to end up in a human trafficking ring or being fostered out to families who just wanted a tax break, never to be seen again.

Katie shook her head to stop from going further down that rabbit hole. From her research, she knew the statistics, and they were dismal. She knew that Jenice was a rare exception to the norm. She suddenly had the urge to check and make sure Jenice was okay. A surge of fear shot through her. What if Jenice had run away? What if someone had come and taken her in the night? Katie quickly ran to Jenice's bedroom door and frantically opened it.

Thank God.

The child was sleeping on her side, slowly breathing in and out. Katie softly came closer to the bed and watched the rise and fall of the blankets. Jenice's face looked at peace for the first time since Katie met her. Gone were the worry lines that no ten-year-old should have, smoothed out by a good night's sleep and a sense of security the child had likely not known in a long time, if ever.

Katie wished Jenice's mom could see her like this. She wanted nothing more than to video call her and show her that her daughter was safe. She placed her hand on Jenice's small shoulder and breathed with her. Jenice's eyes fluttered open after a moment. She looked confused for a second as she took in her surroundings, not remembering where she was until her eyes met Katie's. Jenice smiled and Katie smiled back.

"I didn't mean to wake you," Katie said softly.

"It's okay. I had a good sleep," Jenice replied. "Is Momma here?"

Katie's hand slid to her lap as she sat gently on the bed. Her heart sank a little.

"I'm sorry, sweetie, she is not. I have not heard from her in a while. Remember, she had to go back to El Salvador?"

Sadness and fear entered Jenice's eyes as she recalled the conversation they had at the group home. Katie's heart melted. A child should never wear that look.

"But she's safe, okay? Remember, Aliyah is working with the people down there to help her. So someday soon you can see her again?"

Jenice's eyes lit up a little at the suggestion. "Yes. She is safe. And I can stay here with you. That's what Aliyah said."

"Exactly. You can stay here for as long as you need, Jenice."

Suddenly the child sat up and gripped Katie in a huge hug. She could sense the relief in the child's body as she hugged her back.

"Thank you, Katie," Jenice cried.

Katie smiled warmly, trying to take all of the anxiety she felt from Jenice, trying to comfort her.

"Who's up for pancakes?" The two turned and smiled broadly at Chad, who had been standing at the doorway and watching the exchange. "I think we might even have chocolate chips."

"REALLY?!" Jenice jumped out of bed with bright eyes, a giant smile on her face, and ran past Chad out to the kitchen.

Katie and Chad both laughed out loud as Katie walked over to his open arms.

"I guess someone likes chocolate chips," he chuckled.

"Or pancakes," Katie replied.

"Or BOTH!" Jenice shouted from the kitchen as they could hear her opening cupboards and pulling out pots and pans excitedly.

Katie turned her face toward Chad's and kissed him firmly. He pulled back after a moment with a smile. "Well I guess that makes three of us."

Katie smiled. "Thank you."

Chad smiled sideways. "Well, you haven't tasted the pancakes so don't thank me yet."

Katie continued to look him in the eyes with great compassion. "No, thank you, Chad. For everything. For this." She motioned to Jenice.

He held her gaze. "Katie, thank *you*."

They hugged and made their way into the kitchen where Jenice was now trying to pour flour into a bowl. They laughed as Chad reached over to help her.

"Why don't you grab the beaters, Jenice. I'll pour and you can stir," Chad said happily.

Jenice giggled and nodded her head. Katie breathed another sigh of relief as she watched the scene. However, somewhere in the back of her mind, she knew this was going to be a long, difficult battle to ensure Jenice and her mom's safety. Chad gently reached over and squeezed Katie's hand.

"We've got this," he said softly.

She nodded, trying to quell the sense of fear that continued to nag at her.

Chapter Thirty-Two

Sarah

"If ya try to leave again with my son, I'll hunt you down and kill ya both."

The vapid words stung Sarah as she stood in the doorway in the dark. It was the darkest part of the night, just before the light begins to creep back into the early morning hours. Ben's murderous threat from a few hours ago still hung in the air as she watched her brother James silently carry her son, Joshua, away from her.

He only said he'd come after us if I tried to leave with Joshy. He didn't say anything about Joshua going with someone else.

Sarah tried to rationalize the thought as tears poured down her face. Losing her son ripped her in two. She didn't think she could ever be the same after she had given him one last kiss as he slept in her arms, just before she handed him over to James.

"I'll care for 'im like 'e's me own, Sarah."

"He is now, James. Please, take 'im far from here. Keep 'im safe."

James nodded, a grim look on his face.

"You've go'ta get yerself away from 'ere, too, Sarah. You've go'ta leave this town."

Sarah knew she was in danger, but she only cared for the safety of her son. At this point, she didn't care if she died, as long as her son was alive and well. He would never get that staying with his father, which is why she had made the gut-wrenching decision to give him to her family for guarding. She didn't know if she'd ever get to see him again, but she knew this was the only way to escape the fate her estranged husband had threatened in his drunken rages time and time again.

The last time he had almost beaten her into a coma, and then he had gone after Joshua. She'd managed to cover Joshua with her own body as he kicked her stomach repeatedly. She had been four months pregnant with their second child, and the beating had sent her into a miscarriage so painful and scarring, she didn't know if she'd ever be able to bear children again. Now, two weeks later, and after yet another night of brutal beating and threats, she was stealing away in the night, leaving everything she knew behind, including her son and family, to try to save both their lives. Her family had been begging her for months to leave Ben, but she felt so scared, as if somehow she had been the one to cause all of this because she wasn't a good enough wife or mother. Now she was proving that she wasn't fit to be a mother.

Just like Ma.

The thought was like a knife through her heart. She was leaving her son, just like her mother had left her and all of her siblings. She wasn't strong enough to stay and face the hardships.

"You're no' her, Sarah. Yer leaving yer son to save his life. Ya canno' take 'im with ya. He'll be safer with us for now. She left us because she never wan'ed to be a mother in the first place. Yer *not* her."

It was the last thing James had said to her before he walked away with the only thing in her life that mattered. She slid to the floor, trying to internalize the heaving sobs that so desperately wanted to escape her. She shook, wracked with grief and anger at herself as she watched them disappear around the corner. Her suitcase, the only thing she planned to take with her and the one thing Ben never noticed was gone because she traveled so much for singing gigs, was sitting next to her, packed and ready to go.

Everything else—most of her clothes, her books, her shoes, her toiletries, anything that would tip him off immediately to her disappearance—she'd leave behind. She knew he would be passed out from the amount of alcohol he drank until at least noon. It was a Saturday, and he didn't have to wake for work. She had told him she had a singing gig in Westfordshire Saturday night and her sister would be driving her since she had her own car (thanks to her very rich husband). She said since the gig was late and so far away, she would be staying overnight at her sister's. She knew Ben wouldn't want to go with her like he normally did because the town was several hours away, and he had a football game with his buddies on Sunday. It's what sent him into a rage. Not being able to have eyes on her at all times, not being able to control her, staying with her family when he wasn't there, all of these things set him off. But at the end of the beating, he'd told her to go because he knew her singing gigs brought in money that he needed to keep his drinking habit going. So he said go, but not without the threat that convinced her that what she had just done was the only thing she could do.

It was terrifying, but she had been left with no other choice if she wanted to survive.

She didn't anticipate the level of anguish she would feel in giving her son to her family, however. Now, she didn't really care if she survived or not. She just knew that if she was going to die, she didn't want it to be at the hands of her husband. So she wiped her face with her hand and slowly stood. The morning light was just beginning to peak over the horizon. It looked to be around 4 a.m.

I've got at least eight hours before he stirs.

She wanted to get as far away from him as she possibly could. She had an aunt who lived several hours away that she was planning to stay with as she decided what she would do next. She had been planning to have Joshua there with her, but after the threat from Ben last night, she knew she wouldn't be able to. So she had called her brother, who lived three towns away and next door to their father, and asked him to take him in. She knew they would be able to protect Joshua if Ben came looking for him.

It was the worst phone call she'd ever had to make.

Sarah took one last look at the home she had built. There was no love lost in these rooms. The house held nothing but pain for her. She quickly grabbed her suitcase and softly closed the front door, locking it, and then leaving the key under the mat. She never wanted to see this house again. The fear and anger swelled in her as she turned and began the walk down the street to the car her sister had left on the street for her. It was her getaway car, her opportunity to finally get away from the man who destroyed her life, and her sister had gladly given it to her to keep for as long as she needed.

What a far cry from where we came.

Sarah shook her head as she thought back upon their lives and the journeys they had each taken to end up where they were. Her face darkened again, and a deep sadness set in as she realized she was the only one who hadn't improved her life like her siblings.

Just like Ma.

She approached the dark green Buick and opened the door. The keys were safely tucked in the center console. She threw her suitcase in the passenger seat and felt another stabbing pain as a flash of Joshua's face went through her mind. He was supposed to be sitting next to her. She had failed him in every way a mother could. She hoped that her brother and his wife would be able to do better by him than she ever could.

With a broken heart, she started the engine and pulled into the road with an unknown journey ahead of her. She was alone, completely alone.

Chapter Thirty-Three

Roseamund

Roseamund sat in a heap, in and out of consciousness. The guards came by infrequently in the night and would shout insults at her or spit on her as they walked by. It had been quite a while since the last guard had traversed the space in front of the Cage. She was freezing, shivering in her torn clothing. Her head lolled forward onto her chest as she dreamed fitfully of a different time, a different place. Where she felt warm and safe, loved. A noise in the distance caused her to stir from her intermittent slumber. She opened her swollen eyes, and through the slats of the Cage, she saw fire! She could smell the smoke and hear the shouting loud and clear now. It seemed that there was a fight going on. She drug herself to the front of the Cage and peered through the largest slat. She could see a man, covered in blood, running toward her. She recognized him as one of Lord Turo's men. He approached the Cage and began to remove the rudimentary lock that had been holding her captive. He frantically flung the door open.

"M'lady Roseamund, Lord Turo ordered me to find you and help you escape! He is battling Lord Devaro, but he is injured! We must head into the forest now! I'll show you the way."

He reached a grubby hand toward her and a wave of relief overwhelmed Roseamund for a moment.

"Roseamund! We must go! Please, hurry!"

She hesitated before taking his hand. "Where is Gwendolyn? And Lady Arabella?"

The man's eyes were wild, frantic. "Lady Arabella has barricaded herself in Lord Turo's manor. There are guards all around her and they are defeating Lord Devaro's men. She is safe for now."

Roseamund waited for the man to tell her about Gwen. When he stayed silent, she repeated, "Where is Gwendolyn?"

The man dropped his hand for a moment, a look of sadness in his eyes.

"They have her tied up on the roof of Lord Devaro's manor. We cannot get to her. Lord Turo was able to cut off Lord Devaro before he made it up there himself, but he could not defeat the number of men he had guarding the girl."

The relief that had washed over Roseamund quickly disappeared, replaced by complete and utter rage. She stood but swayed from the beating she had received earlier. The man reached out to steady her and she pushed him off.

"Please, Roseamund, we must leave." His plea went unheard.

Roseamund had one focus now, and that was to save Gwendolyn. It was her fault that Gwen had been captured. She should have forced her to leave days before she had. She righted herself and shut her eyes for a moment, letting the dizziness pass. When she opened them again, the man took a step back, for Roseamund knew the look in her eyes would be one of pure hatred and revenge.

"I will not be going into the forest. I am going to get Gwendolyn."

She took off running toward the fighting. The man could do nothing but follow her, helpless to the will of a woman on the warpath.

As she came closer to the manor, Roseamund could see that an outer house was burning. The shadows of the fighting men created by the flames towered above her as she ran toward the door that would take her to the roof of the main house. She was just about to enter when she heard a guttural scream of pain. She whipped around and her heart fell when she saw the scene in front of her. Lord Turo was on the ground, his sword a few feet away from him, his fighting arm limp, blood gushing from a large wound in his shoulder. Lord Tyrant was towering over the injured man, preparing for what would certainly be the deathblow. Everything moved in slow motion for Roseamund. Without thinking, she made her way over to the two men and placed herself in front of the tip of Lord Tyrant's sword. Just as he was about to heave, he realized what was in front of him and he paused. A smirk replaced his sneer. He lowered his stance.

"So, the bitch who started it all decides to give her life for the sniveling coward who cannot finish the fight."

Roseamund was ready to take the blow. She did not cower. She no longer feared him and it seemed everyone in the vicinity sensed the change as all eyes went to Lord Tyrant, and his movements faltered for a moment. Then his face changed to rage. He grabbed Roseamund roughly and yanked her toward him so that their faces were centimeters apart, his sweat dripped onto her cheek as he spoke.

"You're not going to die, wench. Not yet." He threw her into the arms of two of his guards. "Take her with us. Make sure she cannot escape. Tonight she will get to watch as everyone she cares about loses their lives."

Roseamund screamed, "NOOO!!" and tried to break free of the men, who had her arms solidly bound. She tried kicking them and they tackled her to the ground. They bound her legs as well and stuffed a cloth in her mouth, then carried her, prone position, into the manor house. As she looked back, she could see Lord Turo lying still on the ground, his men tending to him. He looked deathly pale. She prayed his wound was not fatal.

They wound their way up the spiral stairs that led to the roof. Lord Tyrant was huffing as he went, his lungs surely not used to the strenuous activity he'd embarked on this evening. Roseamund's mind was racing.

It became her final desire to hear the last of his rasping breaths, and she hoped she could be the one to end them. He swung the flap to the roof open and heaved himself onto the stone, followed by the two men who were carrying Roseamund. It took them a moment to get her through the door as she was writhing and wriggling, trying to make them lose their grips on her, but it only made them grip her tighter. She was being squeezed so hard she thought they might break her ribs. She became dizzy with the effort and realized if she was going to somehow break free and kill Lord Tyrant, she would need to relinquish her fight right now. She went limp and the men finished shoving her through the door. They propped her up between them, on the stone path Lord Tyrant had specially built just so he could bring people to the roof to throw them off. He turned toward her, putting on what he thought was his best charm.

"That's a good girl. You finally see that behaving is best." He ran a sweaty, meaty finger through her hair, and she jerked her face away from him. He snarled and slapped her.

"Still learning, I see. Maybe this will teach you a better lesson."

He jerked his head toward a guard already on the roof and motioned to bring someone forward.

It was Gwendolyn.

She was not crying. Her face, instead, displayed a look of sheer hatred. The only resistance one could see was how she continuously jerked away from the guard who was bringing her forward. Roseamund's stomach fell.

He's going to throw her off. He's going to kill her.

She had feared his sexual advances toward the young girl, but she never thought he would do this. He desired her too much. It became clear that he was doing it to bait Roseamund. A sense of dread passed through her. This was it. She knew what she must do. She took a deep breath, and a steadfast calm settled over her body. She waited for the right time to try.

"Give her to me."

The guards threw Gwendolyn into the arms of Lord Tyrant, and he gruffly grabbed the back of her neck as he pulled her up straight, her arms tied behind her. He pushed her to the edge of the roof, just as he had done so many countless times before. Just as he had done with Roseamund's mother. This was the first moment Gwen let out a yelp. She glanced down at the people below her before she raised her eyes to the sky, refusing to watch as her death loomed closer.

"This bitch was caught trying to escape our manor!" Lord Tyrant belched out. "She has been giving me trouble for years! Always flirting, toying with me and my men, acting as if she knows her female wiles can get her whatever she wants!"

He spat down on the people below him. Roseamund could see the cook, several of Lord Turo's men, Antonio the stable man who'd helped them, the girl from the kitchen who'd given them away. The last two were in horrible shape. Antonio looked as if he were an inch away from death. He had gashes all up and down his arms and legs; no doubt he had been whipped mercilessly. Blood gushed from a large wound in his head, falling over the hole where his right eye used to be. His left eye did not appear to fare much better.

They've blinded him.

The girl from the kitchen had a blood-stained skirt, making it clear that Lord Tyrant and likely many of his men had had their way with her before beating her into the form she was now. Some of her hair had been ripped out and she was missing teeth. The bruises on her face made it swell so much that Roseamund barely recognized her.

This is all my fault. I've caused their suffering.

For the first time in her life, Roseamund felt the fight leave her. She had been defeated. Lord Giovanni "Tyrant" Devaro had finally beaten her into submission. She slumped in the arms of the guards who held her. A tear trickled down her face. In her effort to save everyone, she had instead resigned all of them to a fate worse than anything they had faced thus far. There was no going back from this. The weight of her guilt caused her to slump even further into the guards' arms. It was a scream from Gwendolyn that brought her back to the moment. She whipped her head up in time to see Lord Tyrant leaning her far over the edge, holding her by her neck, with one arm around her waist to keep her from falling just yet.

"Everyone take a very close look at this little cunt! This is what defying Lord Giovanni Devaro will get you!" He shook her as if he was about to drop her and she whimpered loudly. Clearly, he was not done toying with her.

Please, for the love of God, just do it if you are going to. Make it quick, God. Take her instantly. Please don't let her suffer.

Tears were now pouring down Roseamund's face as she helplessly watched the girl who'd been like a little sister to her dangling on the edge of the precipice. She no longer cared what happened to herself; she just wanted the suffering to end for those she loved.

Suddenly the two guards holding her slid to the ground. She glanced down and saw that their throats had been slit. She began to turn her head to see who had done it when she felt her bonds being cut. No one was looking at her. All eyes were on Lord Tyrant and Gwendolyn.

"Don't turn around. Just go. Roseamund, this is your chance. Get his attention. Make him turn around. I'll be there to grab Gwendolyn. Go now!" There was no mistaking that the whispers came from Lord Turo.

Roseamund felt the cold hard steel of his rapier in her hand. She gripped it firmly, and in one swift movement, they moved together.

"Lord Devaro!!" she shouted loudly. All eyes turned to her.

Everything happened in slow motion from there. She could see Lord Tyrant sneer as he pivoted his body to face her while he loosened his grip on Gwendolyn. Roseamund screamed as she lunged at him, sword fully drawn. In the corner of her eye, she could see that Lord Turo caught Gwendolyn just as she was falling. She noticed, too, that he had managed to take out the other two guards on the roof. As she brought her eyes back to Lord "Tyrant" Devaro's face, she saw in it something she'd never seen before: fear. Sounds began to seep into her consciousness. She realized she was no longer the one screaming. That a collective gasp had come from the crowd below.

She heard a sickly grunt escape from the monster in front of her, and only then did she look down at her hand. It was still holding onto the rapier, which was stuck hilt deep into the chest of the man she had loathed her entire life. His blood was pouring onto her skin. Then she heard it, his rattling, rasping breath as he began to choke on the liquid filling his lungs. She let go of the sword and looked defiantly up at him, directly into his eyes.

"Your turn."

His eyes widened as she pushed him, as hard as she could, off the edge of the roof.

He tried to grab for her.

"N-n-nooooo!"

She yanked herself from his grip as he toppled to the ground, arms flailing, the last of his breath wasted on a cry for help that no one would heed. He landed with a sickly thud in the same spot her mother had, so many years earlier, the sword nailing him to the ground. At the sight of the dead overlord, Lord Turo's men took that as their chance to renew the fight against Lord Devaro's men. Only now, his men were running away, cowards to the end.

Roseamund stood at the edge, looking down, breathing hard. She felt numb. He was finally gone. Somehow, it didn't fill the hole that was still there, left by her mother's murder. At least now, she knew those she loved who were still alive could make a new life for themselves. And that would have to be enough for her. She knew it never would be, though. She was a shell of who she could have become had it not been for the horrible being below.

She felt a gentle hand on her shoulder.

"Lady Roseamund." Lord Turo's eyes met hers.

Slowly her surroundings came into focus again: The dark night lit only by the torches that had been set on either side of the roof to accentuate the failed show Lord Tyrant had been planning. The slight breeze feathering across Roseamund's face as she turned toward Lord Turo. The dirt surrounding his feet, where the scuffle between her and the monster she killed took place. She breathed in the night air, trying to lift the weight that somehow was still on her chest. She could not bring herself to look Lord Turo in the eye, ashamed of who that monster had turned her into: a killer, almost as bad as the evil man himself.

"I'm no lady," she responded.

"But you are." He reached out and placed his fingers under her chin, bringing her face up to meet his, turning his head so that she could not avoid looking him in the eyes. "You are braver than most of my men. You risked your life, time and time again, to save others. You took down the worst being in existence on your own. If that does not warrant the title of Lady, then I must not call myself a Lord."

The words sank in. A Lady. Lady Roseamund. Tears rebelliously slid down her cheeks as she realized that what she had only dreamed about in her life was suddenly now her reality. She only hoped she could live up to the title and bring honor to her beloved fallen mother.

"We can make it official when we make it back to my manor. I will speak to the king myself about your great acts of valor."

Lord Turo stood proudly in front of her. Then his eyes softened.

"I believe there is someone who wishes to speak with you."

He stepped to the side to reveal Gwendolyn. She was glowing in the soft torchlight. A vision of innocence and kindness dressed in tattered and torn garments where the men had been rough with her. She threw herself into Roseamund's arm, tears flowing freely.

"Rose!"

Roseamund received her in a tight hug. She placed her hand on the top of Gwen's head in a motherly fashion and kissed it softly.

"Gwen. Thank God. I'm sorry."

Gwendolyn pulled her head back from Roseamund's embrace, an incredulous look on her face.

"Whatever for? You saved me. You saved all of us!" Gwendolyn smiled and hugged her tightly again. "You will never know how grateful I am, how much I love you. You are like a sister to me. You saved me."

Roseamund took a deep breath. She let the weight of those words wash over her. The shock of what she had just done began to wear off, and she realized she had done it. She began to hear the faint ring of chimes, bells ringing across the region now that the tyrant's reign was over. They were free, because of her.

She had saved them all.

Chapter Thirty-Four

Katie

The bells became louder and louder, waking Katie from her restless dream.

"Katie. Katie!"

She was being shaken awake. She gasped and sat up immediately.

"She saved them all." As the words fell out of her mouth, Katie realized she was no longer on the roof of Lord Tyrant's manor with Roseamund. She took in her surroundings. Her laptop lay open on the bedside table beside her, stacked precariously on top of a pile of books related to border crossing and immigration laws. As she shook the grogginess off, she realized the phone was ringing and that Chad's hand was on her shoulder. She turned her head away from the table as the harsh morning light from the bedroom window flashed in her eyes for a split second.

"Who saved them all? Katie, you were yelling in your sleep. And then your phone started ringing, but I couldn't wake you. Whoever it is has called back like three times in the past three minutes." Chad's face held concern along with a tinge of annoyance at being awoken so abruptly by the noise.

Katie stared at him, confused for a moment. The dream had been so vivid, so real. She had been there. She felt the heat from the burning torches and saw the blood spatter as Lord Tyrant hit the ground with a sickening thud. She shook head again and Chad gently grabbed her hand.

"Sweetheart, are you okay? Should I answer that, or do you want to?" Now he looked truly concerned.

Katie took a deep breath and shook her head once more, giving his hand a squeeze as the ringing of the phone paused for another interval. "No, I'm sorry, Chad. I'll call them back in minute." She turned to him and looked him straight in the eyes. "I dreamed about Roseamund again. She got caught, and nearly died, but in the end, she killed Lord Tyrant and saved them all."

The sun was fully shining on their blue bedspread at this point. Chad picked at a piece of lint on the top of it as he answered, "And by 'them all' you mean . . ."

"She saved every woman and child in her region. She did it." Katie felt the pride well within her. Chad stilled his hand.

"Katie, it was a dream. No one person can save everyone." Katie could see from the concern and confusion on Chad's face that he did not understand.

"No. This happened, Chad. I truly believe I lived this life. I saved them. And I can do it again. I know I can."

Katie quickly slid her legs over the side of the bed and stood. She turned on her computer and saw that she had completed her op-ed, the cursor blinking at the end of the last sentence.

"With this, Chad." Katie held her laptop so Chad could see the writing. He reluctantly looked at it and then at her.

"I mean, it's a start to hopefully what could become change, sweetheart, but I don't want you to get your hopes up. This is a problem that has been happening for far longer than you or I have been alive."

"In this life, yes. But I've saved entire villages before. Chad, this is what I've been missing! This is it!! I am supposed to do this! I'm supposed to save those people who are only looking to better their lives!"

Katie tossed the computer on the bed and walked around, feeling a bit unhinged and angry. She ripped off her sleep shirt and started digging through her drawer for a bra and new shirt to wear. She put on the bra, clasping the back, and threw the shirt over her head. She knew this was what was going to happen, and she needed Chad to understand. As she stood there by the white closet doors tossing pants on the floor, searching for the right pair of jeans, she could feel his gaze upon her. She looked up, ready to fight for what she knew was real, and stopped short because of the look on his face.

He came up behind her and gently wrapped his arms around her, whispering "I believe you."

Katie turned her head back to him, tears in her eyes. "Really?"

He nodded as she turned fully toward him and enveloped him in a hug. They stood there, next to the closet in their bedroom, Katie half-dressed and Chad still in his pajamas, embracing each other truly for the first time in a long time. Just as a spark started to send their hands into places only couples allow each other to go, the phone began to ring again. Both of them stopped. Katie sighed, and Chad laughed softly.

"Raincheck?" The lust and love in his eyes told her she wouldn't have to wait long for him to cash it in.

She nodded and stooped down to pull on the pair of dark blue jeans she'd chosen.

She gave him a soft kiss and walked around the corner of the bed to grab her phone off the nightstand. She looked down at her phone to see who had called her and saw ten missed calls from Aliyah.

"Oh my God!"

Chad startled at her outburst. He came over to her to see what she was looking at, but she was already calling Aliyah back and held up a hand for him to wait for a moment.

He sat down on the bed as she stood and leaned against the white wall behind her. Katie was aware of the stark feeling of the wall as she listened to the ringing of the phone. They hadn't put photos on the wall because they had been waiting to put up photos of Joshua. Its blankness had been a constant reminder of what they had both lost. Katie watched Chad as he sat waiting for her to make her call. She vowed she would make new memories with him and with Jenice and whatever foster children came through their home, and she would hang them on this wall. Katie was pulled from her thoughts as she heard her best friend pick up.

"Aliyah? What's wrong?"

Katie's face went from concern to shock to utter devastation as she listened to what her best friend was saying on the other end of the line.

"No," she whispered.

Chad jumped up and put his arm around her waist. "What?" She pushed him off lightly and stepped away from him, the energy from the moment they had just shared gone in an instant. He reluctantly stepped back and continued to listen to her side of the conversation.

"When? How?" Katie slowly sat down on the bed. She was barely keeping it together. The sun was shining on her bright yellow T-shirt, but she only felt cold as what Aliyah was telling her began to sink in.

"Katie, there was nothing any of us could do. Mariana had called me yesterday, distraught, saying she couldn't be without her daughter anymore, that she was terrified of staying where she was. I tried to calm her. I told her I was working on a short-term visa so she could visit Jenice, but it would be a few more weeks. She said she couldn't wait, that she didn't think she'd survive that long. She'd been receiving threats again from the local gang there. So she ran."

Katie felt like the world was closing in on her. She was having a hard time breathing a full breath. She was vaguely aware of Chad sitting next to her, his hand rubbing her back as he listened in on the faint voice of Aliyah through the phone. She robotically pulled the phone from her head and pressed the speaker button so he could hear her better.

"Katie, she made it all the way to the river, just as she had done with Jenice before. But she didn't have a guide this time, she was alone, and the current was much stronger this time around. They say she made it about halfway across before she was swept away."

A spark of hope lit in Katie's heart. "So she could still be alive? You said swept away, but Jenice said her mom was a strong swimmer. So maybe she was able to grab onto something and make it to the bank—"

"No. They found her body washed ashore about ten miles down this morning. Katie, she drowned. I'm so sorry. I . . . I am so sorry."

A small whimper at the bedroom door drew Chad and Katie out of their horror at the news. Katie felt like she was turning in slow motion as she realized that Jenice was standing in the doorway, having heard what Aliyah had just said.

"Momma?" Jenice cried. Tears were beginning to pour over her cheeks as Katie ran to her and scooped her up in a tight embrace. She held her firmly and began to stroke her hair, taking in all of the wracking sobs as the child shook in her arms. Chad gathered them both in his arms and the temporary family slid to the floor, trying to shield Jenice from the pain she couldn't handle. The phone, forgotten on the bed, was still on, and Aliyah could be heard crying on her end. With one more whispered, "I'm so sorry," the phone clicked off and went silent.

As the sunlight poured into the room, Katie, Chad, and Jenice poured out their pain and love in their small huddle on the carpeted floor.

After what seemed like hours, Jenice's sobs quieted to sniffles. She had cried herself out and looked up, exhausted, at Katie and Chad.

Chapter Thirty-Five

Sarah

Sarah checked herself in the mirror one more time. Her beautiful auburn hair was held up on one side by a glittering hair broach, a glimmering knot of diamonds and sapphires. It was the one gift her mother had ever given her from her own performing days. The diamonds were not real, of course—it was costume jewelry—but for Sarah, it was priceless. It was a reminder that at one time, her mother had loved her, even if for an instant. She'd given it to her when she was four years old, right around the time Sarah had started singing in front of more people than just her family. She remembered her mother always had a special gleam in her eyes when Sarah would sing. She'd let her finish the song and then swoop her up in her arms saying, "Sarah, m' love, one day you'll 'ave wha' I didn't get to 'ave. You'll be the mos' famous singer in t' world. Men'll love ya and women'll wan' t' be ya, and you'll never be wantin' for affection, love, or admiration." Then she'd set her down and they'd dance hand in hand around the living room. It was something Sarah had held onto all these years.

Sarah dropped her eyes to the dresser where they landed on the one photo she had of Joshua. She was holding him close, a rare moment of pure happiness radiating off both of their faces. It was the day they had gone apple picking, just the two of them. It was the first time Joshua had tasted the sweet, crunchy fruit. The moment he bit into that small taste of heaven, his eyes had lit up and he had gone into fits of giggles, which of course sent her into fits of giggles, as well. It was such a joyful memory for her. Then just like that, the memory was replaced with a gnawing pain inside her stomach. An emptiness, like she hadn't eaten for days and nothing she would eat could ever fill that hunger. The guilt and shame of leaving her son settled in once more and she slowly brought her eyes back to her reflection in the mirror.

How could you have let him go?

The accusation swam in her mind every day. She knew she had done the right thing; she received regular updates from her brother about how Joshua was doing—he was thriving—but she could not move past the idea that she was the one who should be sharing those updates. Jealousy and sadness crept into her heart as her breath hitched. She felt tears coming and clenched her jaw and her fists to make it stop.

"This is what is best, for all of us."

She picked up her small blue clutch, decorated with silver beading in swirling shapes, which was sitting on the dresser next to the photo, and pulled out a white handkerchief. It was the last gift her father had given her before she left their town for safety. He had dabbed her tears with it and then placed it in her hand with a gentle but concerned face.

"Keep this. Fer moments like these. Remember yer loved an' 'ave been and will always be loved. Remember tha' Joshua is loved and tha' you're doin' t' right thing. Someday you'll get ta see yer boy again, Sarah. I know't."

He had wrapped her in one of his giant, warm hugs and then let her go with tears in his eyes.

"Go start anew, and we'll make sure yer boy is well taken care of."

She had driven away in that dark green Buick just as the sun started rising out of the east. The pink and yellow hues painted a beautiful backdrop as her father waved goodbye to her, but everything was blurred like an impressionist painting through her tears.

That had been over two years ago. She had left that godforsaken town and moved to the town of Devonshire, eight hours south of where she had left her entire heart. Her eyes hardened as she looked at herself in the mirror. She was a striking beauty, even with the scar that Ben had left under her right eye. The powder blue gown she wore only accentuated her eyes and features. With one final pat to her hair, she picked up her clutch and left the tiny room in the women's boarding house where she lived. She was decked to the nines for her first singing gig in almost two and a half years, and a small burst of excitement made its way through the sadness and guilt.

Maybe Joshua will hear my voice from this night someday.

The event was a lavish party being thrown by a very well-to-do millionaire who had heard her sing once before when he'd stopped in the pub where she used to sing. One day at her work, he happened upon her and recognized her as the singer who had charmed the entire place years before. Immediately, he had asked that she sing at his event, promising a desirable sum of money in return. It was enough that she'd be able to get out of the room where she lived and get her own place. She'd also be able to send the rest to her brother to start a university fund for Joshua. No one in her family had ever been to university, but from what her family told her about how he was doing, he could possibly be the first. Her son was intelligent, smarter than anyone he'd ever seen, her brother wrote her. To be able to send him to college and set him up for a better life was a dream Sarah had not thought achievable until this gig.

This job would be a godsend for her and him. Not only could she afford these things, but the night's performance was to be recorded, and a copy promised to her so she could send it to her son.

As Sarah started the dark green Buick that had brought her to safety, she reflected back on when she'd come to this town. She had arrived in the early evening and gone straight to the boarding house on a tip from her sister. The woman there, Martha, was an old friend of her father's and had stayed in touch through the years. She knew very little about Sarah, only that she was a "friend" of the family and in need of a place to live and a job. Martha had not asked any questions when Sarah introduced herself as Fanny Kent. Instead she gave her a key to her room and a hug. She was a warm, kindhearted woman. As she hugged her, she had whispered to Sarah, "You're not the first girl to hide out here. You do not have to worry. You will be safe here." She had pulled away from Sarah with a gentle squeeze to her arms and gone back around the desk. In a louder, more formal voice, Martha stated the rules of the house and handed Sarah a piece of paper.

"'Tis a local restaurant that needs a good waitress. They'll hire you on my good word, no questions asked." Martha winked as Sarah accepted the paper.

"Thank ya, Martha. Your kindness will not be forgot'en."

Martha showed her to her room and then left her to be with her own thoughts and feelings. The pain was so overwhelming, Sarah had just laid on her side on the bed and cried through the rest of the night. The next day, she'd gotten herself up, dressed, and went out into the world as Fanny Kent. She'd gotten the job and had been working as a waitress at the pub down the lane ever since. This is where the millionaire happened upon her once more. The second he saw her face, he knew it was the singer from years ago. Having never known her name from the first interaction, he didn't blink an eye when she told him her alias. It helped the guise that Sarah had spent the time she'd been in this town working to lessen her accent. Every little change she could make to be less like Sarah and more like Fanny was an aid to keeping her safe from Ben.

Sarah was stopped at the "Halt" sign at the intersection in the middle of her town, just across from a greasy spoon restaurant. She came out of her reverie as she glanced to see if any cars were coming. A large truck followed by a sedan were barreling down the road so she waited as they came by. Just as she was about to press the gas pedal, she noticed a woman inside the restaurant. The resemblance was so striking that it stopped Sarah cold. She crossed the street and automatically just pulled into the greasy spoon parking lot, instead of going straight toward her gig. As she sat there idling in her parking spot, she could not stop staring at the woman through the window. There, on a stool at the counter, sitting facing the window, was her mother. Her mother. The woman who had abandoned her five children when they were barely old enough to walk and talk, let alone care for themselves. The woman who had given them hours of entertainment when she put on her plays or sang and danced with them in their tiny shack. The woman who, when she left on that frigid day so many years ago, stood in the doorway, looked at Sarah, and said, "Ya don't stop singin', Lit'le Bird. Yer light shines brigh'er than anyone else's."

And then she had closed the door and walked away from all of them, never contacting them again.

After a moment, Sarah turned off the car and started to open the door, her anger swelling from a place so deep she felt she could break the door off its hinges. She just wanted to ask this woman how she could have done that. How she could have left them all so young and vulnerable. How she could have *abandoned* an infant still nursing. How she could have abandoned *her*. But then a flash of Joshua came across her memory and she froze. Somewhere, deep down inside, Sarah knew that no answer from this woman would ever satisfy her, but she also knew that this woman had left because she could no longer survive where she had been. She knew that this woman had left because the children were better off without her, no matter how selfish the reasons for leaving were. And in that moment, she understood and hated her mother all at the same time, just as she hated herself. Her body went limp as the realization settled in.

She was her mother.

Sarah scooted back into her car seat and closed the door. Suddenly she couldn't get away fast enough. She revved the engine and squealed out of the parking lot, turning left onto the road to the millionaire's home. It was an hour drive and getting dark. Once again, she was left alone with her thoughts, which were racing.

How could she be here after all these years of not knowing where she went?

The thought raced over and over in her head as Sarah sped along the deserted, narrow, single-lane road. Rain was starting to fall hard, and she could already barely see the street through her tears alone.

I did to Joshua what she did to me. I am a bad mother, just as she was. I failed him, just like she failed me.

She was staring over at the woods to the right. So dark and ominous. She felt as if shadow demons were coming up from the earth, lurking behind the trees, just waiting to grab her, take her to her final judgement. Where did horrible mothers go in the afterlife? Was there even an afterlife?

What if this is it? What if this is all I have and I've ruined it?

Tears overwhelmed her as her foot pressed harder into the accelerator. She was flying down the road, now slick with oil from a lack of rain for months.

Does she ever think of me? Did she ever love me?

She glanced back over at the trees, only to see that no shadows lurked there anymore.

Even the shadow demons don't think I'm worth it. No wonder she left me. She knew I was no good for anything but a song.

The bitterness swept over Sarah like a cloak, enveloping her completely.

And that's not enough.

What brought her out of her reverie was the faint glow of two lights directly in front of her.

That's not right. They shouldn't be right in front of—

Everything happened in slow motion:

Too late she realized that the vehicle in front of her was in the right place, and it was her car that had drifted over to the oncoming lane; she slammed her breaks as the sound of the truck's horn came blasting toward her car; her car began to fishtail out of her control, no matter how much she tried to control the wheel; she knew a collision was imminent.

A crunch of metal against metal and breaking glass exploded into the night air as the two vehicles hit. The truck hit the car almost head-on and slightly to the right, at the passenger side, and Sarah felt the impact.

Then she felt like she was flying, as her body was thrown toward the windshield. She hit the glass still intact in front of her with a sickening thud, and it shattered all around her as she continued through it and ended up sprawled over the hood as the truck and now ravaged car came to a screeching halt. With the final stop of the vehicles, her body rolled completely off the car and landed harshly on the pavement.

She opened her eyes for a brief moment, the lights glaring in her face, and saw a figure coming toward her. She knew her body was broken.

I'm dying.

She had been a fighter her entire life, escaping near-death situations countless times, but this time, she knew, she would not get to see her son again, she would not be able to escape this, and the sadness overwhelmed her.

My son. I love you.

The sun was shining on the small group of people gathered at the cemetery. Sarah once again felt she was a part of the scene, but not. She felt like she was there in a different form. No longer a part of this world, but witness to what was going on in it. When she began recognizing faces, she realized this was her funeral. One by one, Sarah's siblings brought a single calla lily to her pine coffin and placed it on top. Tears flowed freely from Thomas's eyes as he knelt next to the box and placed his forehead on it, gripping the edge with his hands.

"M' child, m' sweet Sarah. Can ye forgive me? I couldn'a protect ye in this life. I'm so sorry! I was try'in t' be the father ye needed n' I failed ye. Bu' I won' fail ye wit' yer son. Li'l Joshua is safe m' luv. He will always be safe. I promise ye. I love ye, my precious child."

The sobs overtook him and Sarah's brother, Leo, came up to pull his father back from the coffin. Thomas leaned heavily on Leo as the two walked back to where they had been standing. They passed little Joshua, quietly holding James's hand, unaware of his mother's fate, that his life would be forever changed because of the love of a woman who risked everything to make sure he would be taken care of. This love could be seen on each of her sibling's faces: Jane, James, Leo, and little Grace, now almost an adult. They were Joshua's family, and they would always be there for him, keeping his mother's spirit in their hearts.

As the preacher concluded his remarks with a prayer, and the people bowed their heads, Sarah became aware of a figure leaning against a tree in the distance. No one noticed her. Silent tears fell as she watched the scene come to an end. When the crowd began to disperse, the woman waited, silently, until everyone was gone except for the men lowering the casket into the earth and then burying it. Only then did she come close to the place where Sarah was laid to rest. She knelt to the earth and placed her hand on the ground in front of her. Her other hand was laid over her heart. Sarah realized who it was . . . her mother, Lillian. Sarah watch as it seemed Lillian was struggling to breathe through her tears.

"M'am, are you a'right?" the groundskeeper asked.

Lillian looked up at him and nodded, waving away his helping hand.

"Did ye know the deceased?" he asked gently.

Lillian looked to the mound of earth where her daughter now lay. A daughter she had abandoned. A daughter she never took the time to get to know. Sarah could see the guilt and grief on her face. She watched Lillian close her eyes for a brief moment, inhale, and let it out.

"Once, a long time ago. She was one a t' best people I knew."

"I'm sorry fer ye loss, m'am." The groundskeeper stepped away softly to give the woman some space.

Lillian sat there for a long time in silence. Finally, her tears dried up. She wiped her face, stood, and with one last glance, she turned and left the graveyard. Sarah watched her go, and as she did, the light around her became brighter and brighter until all Sarah could see now was the light. She felt she was becoming the light. And then, all that existed anymore was light.

Chapter Thirty-Six

Katie

"Katie! Sweetheart, wake up!"

Chad's arms were wrapped around Katie as she woke, drenched in her own tears. She turned into Chad and hugged him back, a sob escaping her.

"It was Sarah, she died again . . . I died again! It's the same dream, Chad! Only this time, I learned why she got so distracted."

She gently pushed off Chad and sat up. He sat up with her, listening with a concerned look on his face.

"Honey, maybe you should talk to that therapist again." He placed his hand on her arm in a gentle motion. Katie moved her arm away and swiftly stood up, throwing the dark blue comforter off her and onto Chad in the process.

"No! No, the therapist would just tell me I need to process what lessons these past lives are trying to teach, what lessons I need to learn in this life. Sometimes they carry over. I didn't know what Sarah's lesson was until just now."

Katie turned back to see Chad removing the comforter from himself, a bemused look on his face. It shifted to concern again when he noticed her looking at him, wide eyed. He sighed, and the look changed to curiosity. Katie took a breath, calm now.

"Sarah spent her entire life running from the mistakes her mother made by neglecting them and then leaving them, only to die thinking she had done the same thing by giving her son to her brother so she could escape that horribly abusive marriage. She thought she had failed her child, just like her mother did, by leaving him. But she didn't just leave him; she was planning to go back for him when things were safe, when she knew she could get him without a threat from her husband. But she never got the chance because she got into that accident. And the reason she got into the accident is because she saw her mother."

Chad's face now wore a look of shock.

"She saw the woman who abandoned them when they were young?"

"Yes." Katie leaned back into Chad, taking up the space between them. She grabbed his hand, an unconscious gesture of security and assurance. "And immediately she jumped to the conclusion that she was just like her. She couldn't see that in giving her son to her family, temporarily, she truly saved him. She died thinking she had failed as a mother."

Chad leaned his head back onto the wall. The sunlight struck a halo around him. "That's some heavy stuff, Katie."

"Yes, it is." Katie joined him, leaning her own head back against the light blue wall they had painted together last year. Last year, when they had decided to repaint all the rooms because they were painting the baby's room. The memory stung and tears welled up in Katie's eyes. "And it's what I've been feeling about *our* Joshua. And I can imagine, it's how Mariana felt about Jenice, why she ended up trying to come get her. We couldn't save our children."

Chad's eyes softened and a glint of a tear formed at the corners. He reached for her hand again, a soft, supportive touch. It was warm and reassuring to Katie. She looked at their hands entwined on the deep sapphire bedspread and marveled at how lucky she was, even amid all the pain of the past year.

"Oh Katie, no one could have saved Joshua. It wasn't your fault." He turned her face toward him with his other hand, wiping away a tear that had escaped down her cheek. His eyes told Katie that he had been feeling just as much pain as she had.

"I know that in my head, but in my heart, I don't know that I'll ever believe that."

The look on Chad's face broke Katie's heart. She squeezed his hand and grabbed the other from her face, bringing them both to a sitting position, hands grasped together, facing each other.

"Which is why we *have* to save Jenice, Chad!" Her intensity was palpable in the room. "We cannot let her go back into the system. We must fight for this adoption! She deserves the life her mother so desperately wanted to give her! And her mother deserves justice! People need to know that she died *saving* her child."

Chad gently placed his hands onto Katie's arms and looked her directly in the eye.

"And so they will. Katie, if anyone can make that happen, it's you. I'll be there right by your side. And of course, of course I want to adopt Jenice. Let's call Aliyah and see what the process is okay? Then we need to ask Jenice if that is what she wants. If it is, then let's do it."

Katie's heart swelled as she looked into the eyes of the man in front of her. She couldn't imagine living this life with anyone else but him. And now, maybe, just maybe, they'd get a chance to live their lives with another who needed the love the most.

Chapter Thirty-Seven

Anya

The air was dense with the scents of the lavender and jasmine that hung from the ceiling. The scents that help to gently encourage the detachment of the soul from its physical form. Anya lay on a palate in the center of the hut, surrounded by geraniums, rose petals, and chrysanthemums. Yaari stood at the pot warming over the fire, dropping dandelion into the boiling water, she seemed distraught over the fact that the cure they had worked so hard to find for the rest of the villagers did not seem to be helping her beloved mentor. As the smoke exited through the hole in the ceiling of the hut, Anya watched with wonder and a deep peace she had not felt in years.

I, too, will soon be released from this earthbound body, into the ether above.

The thought comforted her. Anya knew it was time. Her body, wracked by the same illness that had attacked her people, was no match for what the virus had done to it. She was too frail to fight anymore. She didn't need to fight anymore. She looked over to Yaari and smiled. Her protégé, the daughter she'd never born, but had loved just the same, was finally ready to step into the role Anya had held for a lifetime.

Yaari turned with a bowl full of the dandelion tincture in her hand, ready to make another attempt of saving her hero. Anya reached out a hand to her and whispered, "My child, that will no longer aid me in my journey. Come, set it down, and come to me."

A tear trickled down Yaari's face and Anya watched the struggle in Yaari as she worked to decide if she would heed her leader's request. The suggestion won, and she placed the bowl on the ground and came over to grasp Anya's hand.

"Anya, you saved me. Please, let me save you."

Anya hushed the young woman as Yaari patted her feverish head with a damp cloth.

"My time in this realm is done, my child. No tincture or salve will stop the call of Mother Earth and Father Sky when it is time for a spirit to move forward."

Yaari made to speak, but Anya continued.

"Your time is only beginning, my sweet Yaari. I saw something in you those many years ago when your spirit was trying to leave too soon. You are a fighter. You are a leader. You have the gifts that I, too, possess. It is your turn to lead our people and care for their well-being."

At this, Yaari shook her head. She wasn't ready. She was scared. How could anyone believe she would ever be anywhere close to the leader that Anya was? Anya sensed this fear in her.

"Yaari, hear me. You are already the leader I always wished I could be. You saved the people where I faltered."

"No Mother Anya, we both saved them—"

"*You* are the one who discovered the dandelion root. You are the one who poured it into the mouths of the dying mothers, fathers, and children."

"But you are the one who made it possible to use, Anya!"

Yaari gripped Anya's hand tightly as tears began to flow more freely down her cheeks.

"I am not ready! I cannot do this without you!"

Anya placed her other hand on Yaari's grip and it instantly relaxed.

"Hush, my child. You are not alone. You have your mother. You have your husband. And you have the love, gratitude, and trust of all of our people. That is all a leader needs. You will grow into the role. It took me so long to accept that I was their leader. Even then, anytime I made mistakes, I could not accept that I was fully the one in charge. Until I was able to save you."

Anya reached up with a gentle smile and wiped away the tears on Yaari's face. Yaari leaned into the gesture, closing her eyes for a moment.

"That day was the day I realized I *had* to be the leader, no matter the consequences or struggles, because I knew best what our people needed and how to guide them to it. You will find your way and the people will help you. Trust them in return. Lean on your family. Do not believe that we are ever by ourselves in this journey. Even now, you are here, helping guide my spirit along."

A fresh stream of tears fell at the words, but Yaari nodded in acceptance. She leaned down to Anya and kissed her forehead.

"I will make you as comfortable as possible until your spirit leaves the space."

Yaari stood and headed back to the boiling pot. She scooped out the dandelion and began to drop bits of dried lavender and rose petals into the bowl. Just then, she heard footsteps coming up to the doorway of the hut. She turned in time to see Inchi, her mother, and Amaruq, her new husband, quietly enter the hut. She smiled faintly at them, and in return, Amaruq came over to her and wrapped her in his arms. Anya witnessed Yaari's body sag into her husband's. She knew this moment was hard on her apprentice, but she also knew that Yaari would persevere. Inchi moved to Anya's side and began to pat her head with the damp cloth. The two women quietly spoke to one another, Inchi leaning close to hear the dying woman's final words.

"Thank you for saving my daughter, Anya."

"Thank you for trusting me, Inchi."

They continued their conversation as Yaari lifter her head to Amaruq.

"Anya says I am to lead the village now."

The older women in the room went silent, and Anya saw concern on Inchi's face as she heard the statement, but Anya place a tired hand on Inchi's and gave it an encouraging squeeze. The two women continued to listen to the young lovers.

Amaruq leaned down and kissed Yaari softly.

"My love, do you remember the day I proposed?"

Yaari looked at him quizzically.

"Of course I remember. It was only six months ago."

Amaruq laughed softly.

"I came into the hut, nervous as a scared animal, knowing I wanted to ask you to be my wife. And then I saw you. You were tending to a man who was near death, who was convulsing with death rattles. Something that would have shaken even the strongest warrior to see, and yet, you remained calm. You kept telling him that you were there, that you were going to take care of him. You were confident as you poured the tincture that you and Anya made together into his mouth. It calmed his convulsions almost immediately. And it calmed my nerves, too. Witnessing your strength and confidence in your abilities to care for your people gave me the confidence to know I was doing the right thing by joining with you in a divine union. I walked right over to you—"

"And you thrust a bouquet of dandelions in my face." Yaari laughed at the memory. "I thought you were bringing me more supplies for the tincture!"

They both laughed. The two women in the background were smiling softly.

"And then you asked me to be your wife." Yaari leaned into his strong chest, placing her hand on his heart.

"And without a moment's hesitation, you said yes." Amaruq pulled Yaari back from him slightly and gazed lovingly down at the amazing woman in front of him. "Yaari, you have never second-guessed yourself. You cannot start now. You have your people relying on you to lead them into the future." He turned her toward the scene in front of them: the hut, Anya's beautiful death pyre, the villagers slowly and softly making their way into the hut. Already it was almost full of those wanting to pay their respects to the women who had been guiding them through their trials and triumphs.

Yaari inhaled, taking it all in, glanced back at Amaruq who nodded, and walked back over to where Anya lay. She placed herself opposite of Inchi, and the two women gently held Anya's hands as Yaari began to recite the final death chant of her people.

> *Mother Earth and Father Sky, guide this spirit to her*
> *next destination. Keep her safe as she travels the*
> *spirit realm. Show her love and mercy as her spirit*
> *flies free. Thank you for this soul.*

As Yaari continued her keening, the villagers joined in, from inside and outside of the hut. Everyone was there to show their love and respect for the leader who had saved them and guided them countless times.

Anya gazed at Yaari, a sheen coming over her eyes, a soft smile at her lips.

"I am at peace. I have done what I came to do. I will always be with you, my child."

Yaari leaned into the women and placed a warm hand on her mentor's face. She smiled gently at Anya and whispered, "Thank you."

With that, the life left Anya's eyes and Yaari sensed her spirit leaving her body. A beautiful white light shone in from the hole in the top of the hut and encapsulated Anya's earthly form in a glow as her spirit hovered above for a moment. The villagers' chanting subsided and a peaceful quiet lingered. Then the light diminished.

Anya was gone.

Chapter Thirty-Eight

Roseamund

"Lady Roseamund? Would you like your tea in your room or in the kitchen today?" the young woman asked kindly. "Lady Roseamund?"

Roseamund lifted her head out of the reverie she had been in. "Oh, Annabeth, I'm sorry, I was so deep in thought I didn't hear you."

She smiled softly at the young girl. The girl who had given her away. The girl who, ultimately, had led to the timely death of the Tyrant who had taken her innocence and so many others. Roseamund's smile deepened.

"I'll take my tea in the kitchen. I'd like to chat with Cook about our chickens."

Annabeth giggled a bit. "You mean the escape artists? The little rascals seem to figure out every encasement that Antonio can come up with."

Roseamund laughed at this. "It seems we have some very intelligent poultry on our hands. Maybe we should just let them roam free like the rest of us."

At this, Annabeth quieted and looked downward. She gripped the tray in her hands, her knuckles turning white. Softly she whispered, "Free."

Roseamund placed her hand on Annabeth's cheek and guided her eyes upward. "Free thanks in part to you, dear Annabeth."

Annabeth's eyes shone with guilt and shame.

"Do not ever feel shame for fighting for your life, my dear. Your honesty is one of the things we all love best about you. You never need to feel ashamed of that."

Annabeth went to disagree, but Roseamund cut her off. "Things happened the way they were supposed to. If you had not given us away, Lord Tyrant would still be alive and likely hunting us all down. Your honesty forced us to do what we had needed to all along: face him and take him down. Never, ever apologize for that."

Annabeth's eyes softened with tears, and she nodded and ducked her face away. "I'll take your tea to the kitchen, m'lady."

"Annabeth."

The girl turned back to Roseamund, her face flushed.

"Please, call me Roseamund."

Annabeth nodded again and rushed off, almost knocking into the doorway as she went.

Roseamund shook her head softly. She knew it would take the girl a while to understand that no one held anything against her. They all were just grateful to be alive and free from the Tyrant, Lord Devaro.

In the months following his long overdue death, many things had happened.

Roseamund turned and took in her surroundings. Now in place of the minuscule decorations her room once held, there were floor-to-ceiling bookshelves filled with everything she had requested to learn how to run an estate. She'd had to, since Lord Turo and the king had officially given her the title of Lady and gifted her the lands that she'd grown up on, the lands that once were run by the most despicable man alive. She turned to face the window, running her hands over the plush bedding that now adorned her large poster bed, a gift from Lady Arabella.

"A lady deserves a good night's sleep! You must accept. I insist," Lady Arabella had said as she stood in the doorway with Roseamund weeks ago while her men built the giant four-poster bedframe. Roseamund had felt it to be too extravagant, but Lady Arabella had insisted. "Your people made all the bedding and the mattress, Lady Roseamund. They are falling over themselves to be able to give you everything you never had." As Roseamund went to protest again, Lady Arabella gently squeezed her hand. "You saved them. Let them thank you. Let us all thank you."

Roseamund smiled at the memory. At the woman who was once her kind superior and now was her closest friend. She gazed out the paned window at the land that was now hers. She could see those who'd risked their lives to help her save everyone working away outside. Antonio, the stable man, was wheeling a barrow of hay toward the barn. A young girl was giving chase to the chickens while her mother ran after her, scolding. And then she saw Gwendolyn. The young woman she considered to be her younger sister. The one who'd set the whole plan in motion. Her heart warmed and swelled. Gwen was carrying a basket of wildflowers back from the forest. The sun shone on her beautiful chestnut hair as she walked across the grounds. Roseamund took in the scene with such love in her heart. Only then did she notice Antonio gazing at Gwendolyn with his one healed eye and as much endearment as Roseamund herself.

Now that's something.

Roseamund smiled at the thought of Gwendolyn having a man in her life who loved her as much as it appeared Antonio might. She made a mental note to address the situation with Antonio to see if it were true. Sometimes he needed a little push.

As she continued to reflect upon her people and the generous life she now lived, Roseamund felt a small pang of sadness.

If only Mother had been here to see this.

She breathed with the melancholy moment and let it pass. She knew her mother was with her. She had been the whole time.

With that thought, Roseamund picked herself up and headed out the door into her new life and the joy it would bring.

Chapter Thirty-Nine

Katie

Katie stood in front of what appeared to be a giant wall of flames. Each one as tall as a person, individual in their own silhouettes, she could even make out what appeared to be shapes of faces, yet all of them came together in one giant, bright, shining, canvas of warmth and various shades of golden and copper light. She stood several feet away from the blazing vision, but did not feel like she was burning. She felt safe, supported, and like she was standing in front of something, someone, or many someones that were ancient and yet present all at once. In her head she could hear a faint voice asking her a question.

"And does the wall of flame have a name?"

The voice sounded vaguely familiar, but it was far away, like in a dream. Even though she knew she wasn't dreaming this time. She was very aware of her physical body laying on a soft bed of pillows, covered in a blanket, in a room far, far away. This was her consciousness, her spirit, it must be. She remembered the voice had asked a question. She thought she didn't know the answer, but one look at the face shapes in the wall of fire, one in the center in particular, and right away she knew. They are the Council. My Council. The flame face looked like it nodded in ascent. She could hear her own voice lightly responding

"They are called the Council. They are my spirit guides."

The other voice in the room far, far away responded, "Yes, that's right. And what does the Council do for you?"

Katie turned back to the wall of flame, unsure. The warmth enveloped her and immediately she knew, "They help me find the answers."

Once again, the faraway voice asked, "And what questions do you have?"

Katie didn't think she had any questions, but then she began to think of Roseamund, and Anya, and Sarah. She turned to the Council. "Did I live before? Was I these women?"

The flames flickered and then the one in the center brightened, a clear yes. Katie heard what sounded like a beautiful alto singsong voice reverberate the answer in her head. The sound filled the room. It was the most beautiful thing she had ever heard. It reminded her of her mother's voice. She felt so warm and protected.

"What was I supposed to learn? Why do I keep needing to learn the same thing? Is it about losing children?"

Katie began to feel panicked. She knew she was on to something. The wall of flame still burned as bright as ever, but no answer came. She felt a deep sorrow, as deep as the sorrow she had felt across all of those lifetimes she'd lived. She didn't know the answer, and apparently her Council either couldn't or wouldn't tell her.

Suddenly another being approached from her left.

"It is about losing and finding yourself, Katie."

Katie whipped her head around in time to see Roseamund reach her hand up to Katie's arm in a loving gesture.

"T'is abou' learning how strong ya are. Tha' sometimes the best choice is also the hardest choice." Another set of footsteps approached Katie from her right. She turned to see Sarah, beautiful red hair flowing like before the accident, a kind smile on her face.

"It is about learning what your true gifts are. You are a healer, Katie." The soft, yet strong voice approached her from behind and she felt a gentle hand on her shoulder as Anya shuffled up to stand beside Roseamund. She looked to each of their kind and resilient faces and knew this to be true. A deep understanding blossomed inside of her.

"I am a healer. I am meant to heal the world. I am meant to help others, like Mariana and Jenice."

Anya stepped in front of Katie, the Council at her back, creating a halo around her entire body. "Yes, my child, we are meant to heal the world."

Sarah and Roseamund stepped up next to Anya, each on either side of her, and clasped her hands. The three women stood tall, beautiful, strong, like they had never experienced the horrific things they had in their lives. Katie stood awestruck. How could they be so resilient after everything they had been through? *How could we? How can I?*

"In order to truly heal the world, Katie, you have to understand the pain. You have to experience what it is like to lose, to hurt, to cry. In order to help others, you must go into the pit with them. Only then will they see you and know you are there to help."

The three women now glowed so powerfully with the Council at their backs, it was as if they were becoming a part of the wall of flames. Katie finally understood.

"It was not my fault that Joshua died." The weight of the realization lifted so quickly that Katie felt breathless for a moment.

"No, my child, it was not. Just as it was not my fault that Yaari's father died, or that Roseamund's mother died, or that Sarah had to let go of her own Joshua," Anya answered.

The three women were shifting before Katie's eyes into light themselves. Their voices were becoming more singsong, joining the choir of flames and bell-like voices behind them.

"We were meant to live these lives so we could know how best to love, how best to heal, how best to know ourselves and our true soul," Roseamund said, her voice sounding more like a chime.

"You are tha' soul now, Katie. Just as we are tha' soul. Ever learning, ever growing into more understanding." Sarah sighed sweetly. "It's yer turn to heal."

With that, the women were fully enveloped by the light. Now just face shapes in the wall of individual flames.

"We are all a part of you, as you are of us, child. We will always be here. One day, you will join us. Until then, it is your time to shine." The chorus of voices reverberated in the space, filling Katie's being as she became aware of another voice, far, far away, calling her back with counting.

"Three . . . you're almost to the top of the staircase, two . . . wiggling your toes and fingers, come back into the room, one . . . now you are waking to the scents and sounds in the room, and you are at the top of the stairs. When you are ready, Katie, you may open your eyes. Take as much time as you need to come back to the room."

The familiar sound of Dr. Janet Everwood's voice filled the room.

Katie waited a moment to open her eyes, seeing the light in the room through her eyelids, coming back to total consciousness. As she slowly opened her eyes, she took in her surroundings, the memory of the Council emblazoned in her mind. The room seemed dull compared to the brilliant wall of fire she had encountered in her vision. The soft grays and lavender hues of the room provided the same calming sense they had the last time she was there. It comforted her, much like the comfort she had felt while standing in front of those lighted faces, her spirit Council. As she began to look around more, she noticed small things she had not before—a pink crystal on the table beside her, the doctor's small but beautifully carved desk in the corner, the tapestry hanging from the ceiling. Everything handpicked to fit into this space, curated for the clients to have their best experience.

"How was your journey this time, Katie?"

The doctor's voice brought Katie's vision fully into focus, along with her other senses. Suddenly everything was vibrant, present, alive.

"It was . . . surreal." Katie sat up and hugged the soft blanket closer to her as she struggled to find the words to describe the experience she'd just had.

Dr. Janet looked down to her notes for a brief moment and then back up. "You mentioned you were visiting with your spirit guides, the Council as you've called them in past sessions. What form did they take this time? Were they still the wall of flame as you've described before?

The doctor seemed excited and genuinely interested in what the answer might be.

Katie took a moment to gather her thoughts and spoke, "Yes, they were the wall of flames with face-like shapes again, as if there were many spirits within the one wall."

Katie realized she was petting the blanket in a self-soothing motion. Dr. Janet noticed, as well.

"And did the wall scare you this time?"

"No, not at all. The opposite, actually. I felt they were there only to support and protect me, but not impede upon my free will. If that makes any sense."

Dr. Janet smiled and set down her notebook on the small wooden table next to her. She clasped her hands gently in her lap.

"It makes complete sense. Many of my clients experience this kind of connection with their spirit guides."

Katie sat up a bit straighter, letting the blanket fall to her lap. "Other people have Councils, too?"

Dr. Janet's smile broadened. "Yes. In fact, in my experience, every single person who has walked into this room has left realizing they have spirit guides. I, myself, have experienced a meeting with my guides."

Katie sighed with relief. Somehow, it made her feel more human, more connected, to know that the expert in front of her had the same outer-realm experience. "You have a Council?"

"For me, it's more like I feel surrounded by the stars of the Universe. That I am connected to them as they are to me and that we are all there together. It's how I realized this was my calling. The first time I connected to my guides made me realize my purpose. Some people call them angels. I like to think of them as fellow lightworkers, doing their work from the spiritual realm while I am here doing my work from the earthly realm."

Katie took it in for a moment. Doing her work from the earthly realm. Just like Anya, Roseamund, and Sarah had been trying to do. They all had, in their own way, been trying to help those they loved. Just as Katie was trying to do now with Jenice and, on a larger scale, with her op-ed.

"Lightworkers."

Dr. Janet smiled again. She leaned in toward Katie a bit. "It seems, maybe, you've discovered your purpose while you've been here, too."

Katie looked the woman in the eye and nodded.

"Yes, I believe I have."

Epilogue

For ten years, Katie, Chad, and Jenice worked tirelessly to bring to fruition what Katie had hoped would happen when she wrote her initial op-ed about the treatment of immigrants, particularly woman and children, at the border, as well as immigration law and the path to citizenship overall. The tremendous response to the op-ed had sparked debate all over the country. With the resources of the paper she worked for, she and a team of journalists researched and wrote a major investigative report that went on to win a Pulitzer. Later, with the encouragement of her editor Sam, Katie went on to write a book about her experience with finding, fostering, and eventually adopting Jenice. Jenice even wrote her own perspective, and it was included in the book.

From there, the book took off, causing the entire country to move the needle of change toward immigration. First with conversation, then with demonstrations and action in the form of committees created in every state to address the issues surrounding the treatment of immigrants and immigration law. The issue, being as complex as it is, was hotly discussed in media, in forums, and eventually in congress.

Things moved slowly in congress regarding the numerous bills that were trying to be passed regarding changes to immigration law. So Katie, Chad, and Aliyah took it upon themselves to start a foundation to help family members of displaced immigrants reunite with their family. They took the battles into the justice system in hopes that what happened to Jenice and her mother would never have to happen again to anyone else, regardless of their citizenship status. It was a long, hard, and arduous road toward any wins in court, but eventually, immigrant families started to be reconnected with their kin, and many were able to seek asylum from their war- and gang-ravaged countries.

Which led to why Katie, Chad, and Jenice were standing on the steps of the United States Capitol, listening to the Speaker of the House and Senate Majority Leader address the nation today. Both houses of congress had finally come to a consensus on a bill that would help so many displaced immigrants find a path to citizenship and reunification with their children.

Katie gazed out upon the thousands of people gathered in front of the Capitol, listening to the speech. It was a crystal-clear, blue-sky day. There was a light breeze, and the sun shone upon the crowd like a halo. It reminded Katie of her spirit guides. She smiled. She knew that the spirits of Anya, Roseamund, Sarah, and all of her guides had been with her through this journey and were with her today. Tears of joy welled up in her eyes at the thought.

Chad, who was standing next to her holding her hand, squeezed her hand gently. She turned her face toward him.

"You okay?" He had a look of concern on face. So like the look he'd had anytime he thought she was sad or hurting. Her smile broadened.

"These are happy tears." Katie, who had been holding Jenice's hand with her other hand, unclasped and wrapped her arm around Jenice in a side hug, drawing her closer.

Jenice stopped listening to the speech for a moment and turned toward Katie and Chad. Katie still could not believe what a beautiful young woman Jenice had grown into. It made her heart swell.

"I'm so glad they are happy tears, Katie. Mine are too." Jenice smiled through her tears as they fell upon her face.

Katie leaned in and kissed her cheek. "You are safe. You are loved. Your mother would be so proud of you, Jenice."

Katie and Jenice gazed at each other for a moment, so many things passing between them, unspoken but understood. Katie turned back to Chad and pulled him into a side hug on her other side, bringing the family into a hug.

"We are safe. We are loved."

The three pulled out of the hug and back into the line they had been standing in before, holding hands with each other and listening to the last words from the speech. Out in the distance, Katie could make out what seemed like three figures standing under a tree. Three women, glowing in the sunlight.

Katie smiled and whispered, "We are all here."

Author's Note

This book began as a way to make sense of a past life regression session I experienced in 2017 in Los Angeles. I'd been having a recurring dream about my own death, set sometime in the late 1960s. In the dream, I was wearing a powder-blue dress, I had red hair, and I was a singer. I knew my death was caused by a car accident. I was on the road in the rain, my head in a stranger's lap as he held my hand. And then, nothing. I've had this same dream for as long as I can remember, with my earliest memory of waking from it at about five years old. Since then, I would experience this dream at least two or three times a year. In 2016, it started happening more frequently, and I kept sensing that this wasn't the only life I'd lived.

Around that time, I was also coming to terms with the reality that I couldn't safely bear children. My husband and I had looked into fostering and adoption, but the costs were prohibitive for us. So, I found myself wondering what direction my life should take if motherhood wasn't meant to be part of my path. My husband encouraged me to talk to someone about it, and my therapist suggested that I meet with a hypnotherapist specializing in past life regression. It just so happened that I knew someone who practiced this kind of therapy: Jourdan Rystrom. I met with her, and that day changed my life.

The stories in this novel are inspired by the women I remembered during that session. Jourdan recorded everything I said, so I had a lot of notes to work from. When I woke up, I felt certain that my soul had lived those lives. Coming from a religious background, this revelation was confusing, but I couldn't deny the truth I felt. My heart simply knew. Over the following years, I researched past lives, past life regression therapy, different spiritual perspectives on reincarnation, and did a lot of soul-searching. Writing this book was what truly helped me work through it all.

I'm not the same person I was when I began this journey, which was guided by intuitive nudges I believe came from my Higher Power. Whether this aligns with your own beliefs isn't for anyone to judge—it's just my truth. At the core, the message is universal: finding one's purpose and surrendering to it can lead to a deeper sense of peace.

Writing these experiences in a fictionalized form, especially through the character of Katie, allowed me to process the truths behind these stories. My hope is that this book might encourage you to explore your own beliefs and perhaps bring peace to anyone who might be in a place of questioning.

Acknowledgments

To call this an undertaking is an understatement. I wasn't sure I'd ever write a book, but I knew I had at least one (maybe more) in me. Thanks to the encouragement of many wonderful people, I've finally written my first book, and I couldn't be more grateful. Transitioning from screen-writing to novel writing has been a journey, and I couldn't have done it without the support of so many.

First and foremost, I owe endless thanks to my husband, my unwavering cheerleader in all my creative pursuits, but especially with this book. Without your encouragement to finish and put it out into the world, this book wouldn't exist. To my dad, my sister, and my mother-in-law, thank you for reading, giving feedback, and then reading it all over again (especially to my sister, who also took on the final proofread)! And thank you to my amazing beta readers, whose insights helped shape this story into what it is now. To all my family and friends—thank you for standing by me, cheering on my wild ideas, and helping me see them through, even when the going gets tough. You've all been incredible, especially you, Mom and Dad.

A special thank-you to Jourdan Rystrom, hypnotherapist and past life regression therapy specialist. I wouldn't have learned as much about myself or these women without stepping into your office that fateful day in Los Angeles. Thank you for guiding me in discovering these parts of myself and for helping me make sense of the recurring dreams and nudges I've felt throughout my life.

A huge thank-you to Nicole Frail. This book would be a shadow of itself without your expert editing and typesetting skills. Your thoughtful suggestions helped make this the best it could be, and your encouragement has meant so much.

And thank you to Oh So Novel for the beautiful cover art. Mignon, you turned my jumbled descriptions into something truly remarkable.

Of course, I'd be remiss if I didn't thank our six cats for their "support" during this process. Marigold, our orange tabby queen (who would write me off entirely if I didn't recognize her contributions), has been especially dedicated to her role—walking all over my keyboard and tirelessly attempting to divert my attention away from "the book." So thank you, Marigold, Honey, Obi, Major Tom, Yoshi, and Joygie, for your endless patience and furry companionship. But especially Marigold, because, let's be real, she wouldn't have it any other way.